GULLIVER'S TRAVELS

Jonathan Swift

PART I: A VOYAGE TO LILLIPUT.

CHAPTER I.

The Author Gives Some Account of Himself and Family: His First Inducements to Travel. He is Shipwrecked, and Swims for His Life; Gets Safe Ashore in the Country of Lilliput; is Made a Prisoner, and Carried Up the Country.

My father had a small estate in Nottinghamshire; I was the third of five sons. He sent me to Emmanuel College in Cambridge at fourteen years old, where I resided three years, and applied myself close to my studies; but the charge of maintaining me, although I had a very scanty allowance, being too great for a narrow fortune, I was bound apprentice to Mr. James Bates, an eminent surgeon in London, with whom I continued four years; and my father now and then sending me small sums of money, I laid them out in learning navigation, and other parts of the mathematics useful to those who intend to travel, as I always believed it would be, some time or other, my fortune to do. When I left Mr. Bates, I went down to my father, where, by the assistance of him, and my uncle John and some other relations, I got forty pounds,[2] and a promise of thirty pounds a year, to maintain me at Leyden. There I studied physic two years and seven months, knowing it would be useful in long voyages.

Soon after my return from Leyden, I was recommended by my good master, Mr. Bates, to be surgeon to the "Swallow," Captain Abraham Pannell, commander; with whom I continued three years and a half, making a voyage or two into the Levant,[3] and some other parts. When I came back I resolved to settle in London; to which Mr. Bates, my master, encouraged me, and by him I was recommended to several patients. I took part of a small house in the Old Jewry; and, being advised to alter my condition, I married Mrs. Mary Burton,[4] second daughter to Mr. Edmund Burton, hosier in Newgate Street, with whom I received four hundred pounds for a portion.

But my good master, Bates, dying in two years after, and I having few friends, my business began to fail; for my conscience would not suffer me to imitate the bad practice of too many among my brethren. Having, therefore, consulted with my wife, and some of my acquaintance, I determined to go again to sea. I was surgeon successively in two ships, and made several voyages, for six years, to the East and West Indies, by which I got some addition to my fortune. My hours of leisure I spent in reading the best authors, ancient and modern, being always provided with a good number of books; and, when I was ashore, in observing the manners and dispositions of the people, as well as learning their language, wherein I had a great facility, by the strength of my memory.

The last of these voyages not proving very fortunate, I grew weary of the sea, and intended to stay at home with my wife and family. I removed from the Old Jewry to Fetter Lane, and from thence to Wapping, hoping to get business among the sailors; but it would not turn to account. After three years' expectation that things would mend, I accepted an advantageous offer from Captain William Prichard, master of the "Antelope," who was making a voyage to the South Sea.[5] We set sail from Bristol, May 4, 1699; and our voyage at first was very prosperous.

It would not be proper, for some reasons, to trouble the reader with the particulars of our adventures in those seas. Let it suffice to inform him, that, in our passage from thence to the East Indies, we were driven by a violent storm, to the northwest of Van Diemen's Land.[6]

By an observation, we found ourselves in the latitude of 30 degrees and 2 minutes south. Twelve of our crew were dead by immoderate labor and ill food; the rest were in a very weak condition.

On the fifth of November, which was the beginning of summer in those parts, the weather being very hazy, the seamen spied a rock within half a cable's length of the ship;[7] but the wind was so strong, that we were driven directly upon it, and immediately split. Six of the crew, of whom I was one, having let down the boat into the sea, made a shift to get clear of the ship and the rock. We rowed, by my computation, about three leagues, till we were able to work no longer, being already spent with labor, while we were in the ship. We, therefore, trusted ourselves to the mercy of the waves; and, in about half an hour, the boat was overset by a sudden flurry from the north. What became of my companions in the boat, as well as those who escaped on the rock, or were left in the vessel, I cannot tell, but conclude they were all lost.

For my own part, I swam as fortune directed me, and was pushed forward by wind and tide. I often let my legs drop, and could feel no bottom; but, when I was almost gone, and able to struggle no longer, I found myself within my depth; and, by this time, the storm was much abated.

The declivity was so small that I walked near a mile before I got to the shore, which I conjectured was about eight o'clock in the evening. I then advanced forward near half a mile, but could not discover any sign of houses or inhabitants; at least, I was in so weak a condition, that I did not observe them. I was extremely tired, and with that, and the heat of the weather, and about half a pint of brandy that I drank as I left the ship, I found myself much inclined to sleep. I lay down on the grass, which was very short and soft, where I slept sounder than ever I remembered to have done in my life, and, as I reckoned, about nine hours; for, when I awaked, it was just daylight. I attempted to rise, but was not able to stir: for as I happened to lie on my back, I found my arms and legs were strongly fastened on each side to the ground; and my hair, which was long and thick, tied down in the same manner. I likewise felt several slender ligatures across my body, from my arm-pits to my thighs. I could only look upwards, the sun began to grow hot, and the light offended my eyes.

I heard a confused noise about me; but, in the posture I lay, could see nothing except the sky. In a little time, I felt something alive moving on my left leg, which, advancing gently forward over my breast, came almost up to my chin; when, bending my eyes downward, as much as I could, I perceived it to be a human creature, not six inches high, with a bow and arrow in his hands, and a quiver at his back. In the meantime I felt at least forty more of the same kind (as I conjectured) following the first.

I was in the utmost astonishment, and roared so loud that they all ran back in a fright; and some of them, as I was afterwards told, were hurt with the falls they got by leaping from my sides upon the ground. However, they soon returned, and one of them, who ventured so far as to get a full sight of my face, lifting up his hands and eyes by way of admiration, cried out in a shrill, but distinct voice—*Hekinah degul!* the others repeated the same words several times, but I then knew not what they meant.

I lay all this while, as the reader may believe, in great uneasiness. At length, struggling to get loose, I had the fortune to break the strings, and wrench out the pegs, that fastened my left arm to the ground; for by lifting it up to my face, I discovered the methods they had taken to bind me, and, at the same time, with a violent pull, which gave me excessive pain, I a little loosened the strings that tied down my hair on the left side, so that I was just able to turn my head about two inches.

But the creatures ran off a second time, before I could seize them; whereupon there was a great shout in a very shrill accent, and after it ceased, I heard one of them cry aloud, *Tolgo phonac*; when, in an instant, I felt above an hundred arrows discharged on my left hand, which pricked me like so many needles; and, besides, they shot another flight into the air, as we do bombs in Europe, whereof many, I suppose, fell on my body (though I felt them not), and some on my face, which I immediately covered with my left hand.

When this shower of arrows was over, I fell a-groaning with grief and pain, and then striving again to get loose, they discharged another volley larger than the first, and some of them attempted with spears to stick me in the sides; but by good luck I had on me a buff jerkin,[8] which they could not pierce. I thought it the most prudent method to lie still, and my design was to continue so till night, when, my left hand being already loose, I could easily free myself; and as for the inhabitants, I had reason to believe I might be a match for the greatest army they could bring against me, if they were all of the same size with him that I saw.

"I LAY ALL THIS WHILE IN GREAT UNEASINESS"

But fortune disposed otherwise of me. When the people observed I was quiet, they discharged no more arrows: but, by the noise I heard, I knew their numbers increased; and about four yards from me, over against my right ear, I heard a knocking for above an hour, like that of people at work; when, turning my head that way, as well as the pegs and strings would permit me, I saw a stage erected, about a foot and a half from the ground, capable of holding four of the inhabitants, with two or three ladders to mount it; from whence one of them, who seemed to be a person of quality, made me a

long speech, whereof I understood not one syllable.

But I should have mentioned, that before the principal person began his oration, he cried out three times, *Langro debul san* (these words, and the former, were afterwards repeated, and explained to me). Whereupon immediately about fifty of the inhabitants came and cut the strings that fastened the left side of my head, which gave me the liberty of turning it to the right, and of observing the person and gesture of him that

6

was to speak. He appeared to be of a middle age, and taller than any of the other three who attended him, whereof one was a page that held up his train, and seemed to be somewhat longer than my middle finger; the other two stood one on each side, to support him. He acted every part of an orator, and I could observe many periods of threatenings, and others of promises, pity, and kindness.

I answered in a few words, but in the most submissive manner, lifting up my left hand, and both my eyes, to the sun, as calling him for a witness: and, being almost famished with hunger, having not eaten a morsel for some hours before I left the ship, I found the demands of nature so strong upon me, that I could not forbear showing my impatience (perhaps against the strict rules of decency) by putting my finger frequently to my mouth, to signify that I wanted food. The *hurgo* (for so they call a great lord, as I afterwards learned) understood me very well. He descended from the stage, and commanded that several ladders should be applied to my sides; on which above a hundred of the inhabitants mounted, and walked towards my mouth, laden with baskets full of meat, which had been provided and sent thither by the king's orders, upon the first intelligence he received of me.

I observed there was the flesh of several animals, but could not distinguish them by the taste. There were shoulders, legs, and loins, shaped like those of mutton, and very well dressed, but smaller than the wings of a lark. I ate them by two or three at a mouthful, and took three loaves at a time, about the bigness of musket bullets. They supplied me as they could, showing a thousand marks of wonder and astonishment at my bulk and appetite. I then made another sign that I wanted drink.

They found by my eating that a small quantity would not suffice me; and being a most ingenious people, they slung up with great dexterity, one of their largest hogsheads, then rolled it towards my hand, and beat out the top: I drank it off at a draught; which I might well do, for it did not hold half a pint, and tasted like a small[9] wine of Burgundy, but much more delicious. They brought me a second hogshead, which I drank in the same manner, and made signs for more; but they had none to give me.

When I had performed these wonders, they shouted for joy, and danced upon my breast, repeating, several times, as they did at first, *Hekinah degul.* They made me a sign, that I should throw down the two hogsheads, but first warning the people below to stand out of the way, crying aloud, *Borach nevola*; and, when they saw the vessels in the air, there was an universal shout of *Hekinah degul.*

I confess, I was often tempted, while they were passing backwards and forwards on my body, to seize forty or fifty of the first that came in my reach, and dash them against the ground. But the remembrance of what I had felt, which probably might not be the worst they could do, and the promise of honor I made them—for so I interpreted my submissive behavior—soon drove out those imaginations. Besides, I now considered myself as bound, by the laws of hospitality, to a people who had treated me with so much expense and magnificence. However, in my thoughts I could not sufficiently wonder at the intrepidity of these diminutive mortals, who durst venture to mount and walk upon my body, while one of my hands was at liberty, without trembling

at the very sight of so prodigious a creature, as I must appear to them.

"PRODUCING HIS CREDENTIALS."

After some time, when they observed that I made no more demands for meat, there appeared before me a person of high rank from his imperial majesty. His excellency, having mounted on the small of my right leg, advanced forwards up to my face, with about a dozen of his retinue: and, producing his credentials under the signet–royal,[10] which he applied close to my eyes, spoke about ten minutes, without any signs of anger, but with a kind of determinate resolution, often pointing forwards, which, as I afterwards found, was towards the capital city, about half a mile distant, whither it was agreed by his majesty in council that I must be conveyed. I answered in few words, but to no purpose, and made a sign with my hand that was loose, putting it to the other (but over his excellency's head, for fear of hurting him or his train) and then to my own head and body, to signify that I desired my liberty.

It appeared that he understood me well enough, for he shook his head by way of disapprobation, and held his hand in a posture to show that I must be carried as a prisoner. However, he made other signs, to let me understand that I should have meat and drink enough, and very good treatment. Whereupon I once more thought of attempting to break my bonds; but again, when I felt the smart of their arrows upon my face and hands, which were all in blisters, and many of the darts still sticking in them, and observing, likewise, that the number of my enemies increased, I gave tokens to let them know, that they might do with me what they pleased. Upon this the *hurgo* and his train withdrew, with much civility, and cheerful countenances.

Soon after, I heard a general shout, with frequent repetitions of the words, *Peplom selan*, and I felt great numbers of people on my left side, relaxing the cords to such a degree, that I was able to turn upon my right, and to get a little ease. But, before this, they had daubed my face and both my hands with a sort of ointment very pleasant to the smell, which, in a few minutes, removed all the smart of their arrows. These circumstances, added to the refreshment I had received by their victuals and drink, which were very nourishing, disposed me to sleep. I slept about eight hours, as I was afterwards assured; and it was no wonder, for the physicians, by the emperor's order, had mingled a sleepy potion in the hogsheads of wine.

It seems that, upon the first moment I was discovered sleeping on the ground after my landing, the emperor had early notice of it, by an express; and determined in council, that I should be tied in the manner I have related (which was done in the night, while I slept), that plenty of meat and drink should be sent to me, and a machine prepared to carry me to the capital city.

This resolution, perhaps, may appear very bold and dangerous, and I am confident would not be imitated by any prince in Europe, on the like occasion. However, in my opinion, it was extremely prudent, as well as generous; for, supposing these people had endeavored to kill me with their spears and arrows, while I was asleep, I should certainly have awaked with the first sense of smart, which might so far have roused my rage and strength, as to have enabled me to break the strings wherewith I was tied; after which, as they were not able to make resistance, so they could expect no mercy.

These people are most excellent mathematicians, and arrived to a great perfection in mechanics, by the countenance and encouragement of the emperor, who is a renowned patron of learning. The prince hath several machines fixed on wheels for the carriage of trees, and other great weights. He often builds his largest men of war, whereof some are nine feet long, in the woods where the timber grows, and has them carried on these engines three or four hundred yards to the sea. Five hundred carpenters and engineers were immediately set to work, to prepare the greatest engine they had. It was a frame of wood, raised three inches from the ground, about seven feet long and four wide, moving upon twenty-two wheels. The shout I heard was upon the arrival of this engine, which, it seems, set out in four hours after my landing. It was brought parallel to me, as I lay. But the principal difficulty was, to raise and place me in this vehicle.

Eighty poles, each of one foot high, were erected for this purpose, and very strong cords, of the bigness of packthread, were fastened by hooks to many bandages, which the workmen had girt round my neck, my hands, my body, and my legs. Nine hundred of the strongest men were employed to draw up these cords by many pulleys fastened on the poles; and thus, in less than three hours, I was raised and slung into the engine, and tied fast.

All this I was told; for, while the whole operation was performing, I lay in a profound sleep, by the force of that soporiferous medicine infused into my liquor. Fifteen hundred of the emperor's largest horses, each about four inches and a half high, were employed to draw me towards the metropolis, which, as I said, was half a mile distant.

About four hours after we began our journey, I awaked, by a very ridiculous accident; for, the carriage being stopt a while, to adjust something that was out of order, two or three of the young natives had the curiosity to see how I looked, when I was asleep. They climbed up into the engine, and advancing very softly to my face, one of them, an officer in the guards, put the sharp end of his half-pike[11] a good way up into my left nostril, which tickled my nose like a straw, and made me sneeze violently; whereupon they stole off, unperceived, and it was three weeks before I knew the cause of my awaking so suddenly.

We made a long march the remaining part of the day, and rested at night with five hundred guards on each side of me, half with torches, and half with bows and arrows, ready to shoot me, if I should offer to stir. The next morning, at sunrise, we continued our march, and arrived within two hundred yards of the city gates about noon. The emperor, and all his court, came out to meet us; but his great officers would by no means suffer his majesty to endanger his person, by mounting on my body.

At the place where the carriage stopt, there stood an ancient temple, esteemed to be the largest in the whole kingdom, which, having been polluted some years before by an unnatural murder, was, according to the zeal of those people, looked upon as profane, and therefore had been applied to common use, and all the ornaments and furniture carried away. In this edifice it was determined I should lodge. The great gate, fronting to the north, was about four feet high, and almost two feet wide, through which I could easily creep. On each side of the gate was a small window, not above six inches from the ground; into that on the left side the king's smith conveyed four score and eleven chains, like those that hang to a lady's watch in Europe, and almost as large, which were locked to my left leg with six-and-thirty padlocks.

Over against this temple, on the other side of the great highway, at twenty feet distance, there was a turret at least five feet high. Here the emperor ascended, with many principal lords of his court, to have an opportunity of viewing me, as I was told, for I could not see them. It was reckoned that above an hundred thousand inhabitants came out of the town upon the same errand; and, in spite of my guards, I believe there could not be fewer than ten thousand, at several times, who mounted my body, by the help of ladders. But a proclamation was soon issued, to forbid it, upon pain of death.

When the workmen found it was impossible for me to break loose, they cut all the strings that bound me; whereupon I rose up, with as melancholy a disposition as ever I had in my life. But the noise and astonishment of the people, at seeing me rise and walk, are not to be expressed. The chains that held my left leg were about two yards long, and gave me not only the liberty of walking backwards and forwards in a semi-circle, but, being fixed within four inches of the gate, allowed me to creep in, and lie at my full length in the temple.

[2] *Pound*: nearly five dollars.

[3] *Levant*: the point where the sun rises. The countries about the eastern part of the Mediterranean Sea and its adjoining waters.

[4] *Mrs.*: it was formerly the custom to call unmarried women Mrs.

[5] *The South Sea*: the Pacific Ocean.

[6] *Van Diemen's Land*: N.W. from Van Diemen's Land (Tasmania) and in latitude 30 degrees 2 minutes would be in Australia or off the West Coast.

[7] *Cable's length*: about six hundred or seven hundred feet.

[8] *Buff jerkin*: a leather jacket or waistcoat.

[9] *Small*: weak, thin.

[10] *Signet-royal*: the king's seal.

[11] *Half-pike*: a short wooden staff, upon one end of which was a steel head.

Chapter II.

The Emperor of Lilliput, Attended by Several of the Nobility, Comes to See the Author in His Confinement. the Emperor's Person and Habit Described. Learned Men Appointed to Teach the Author Their Language. He Gains Favor by His Mild Disposition. His Pockets Are Searched, and His Sword and Pistols Taken From Him.

When I found myself on my feet, I looked about me, and must confess I never beheld a more entertaining prospect. The country around, appeared like a continued garden, and the enclosed fields, which were generally forty feet square, resembled so many beds of flowers. These fields were intermingled with woods of half a stang,[12] and the tallest trees, as I could judge, appeared to be seven feet high. I viewed the town on my left hand, which looked like the painted scene of a city in a theatre.

The emperor was already descended from the tower, and advancing on horseback towards me, which had like to have cost him dear; for the beast, though very well trained, yet wholly unused to such a sight, which appeared as if a mountain moved before him, reared up on his hind feet. But that prince, who is an excellent horseman, kept his seat, till his attendants ran in and held the bridle, while his majesty had time to dismount.

When he alighted, he surveyed me round with great admiration, but kept without the length of my chain. He ordered his cooks and butlers, who were already prepared, to give me victuals and drink, which they pushed forward in a sort of vehicles upon wheels, till I could reach them. I took these vehicles, and soon emptied them all; twenty of them were filled with meat; each afforded me two or three good mouthfuls. The empress and young princes of the blood of both sexes, attended by many ladies, sat at some distance in their chairs;[13] but upon the accident that happened to the emperor's horse, they alighted, and came near his person, which I am now going to describe. He is taller, by almost the breadth of my nail, than any of his court, which alone is enough to strike an awe into the beholders. His features are strong and masculine, with an Austrian lip and arched nose, his complexion olive, his countenance erect, his body and limbs well proportioned, all his motions graceful, and his deportment majestic. He was then past his prime, being twenty-eight years and three-quarters old, of which he had reigned about seven in great felicity, and generally victorious. For the better convenience of beholding him, I lay on my side, so that my face was parallel to his, and he stood but three yards off. However, I have had him since many times in my hand, and therefore cannot be deceived in the description.

His dress was very plain and simple, and the fashion of it between the Asiatic and the European; but he had on his head a light helmet of gold, adorned with jewels, and a plume an the crest.[14] He held his sword drawn in his hand, to defend himself, if I should happen to break loose; it was almost three inches long; the hilt and scabbard were gold, enriched with diamonds. His voice was shrill, but very clear and articulate, and I could distinctly hear it, when I stood up.

The ladies and courtiers were all most magnificently clad; so that the spot they stood upon seemed to resemble a petticoat spread on the ground, embroidered with figures of gold and silver. His imperial majesty spoke often to me, and I returned answers, but neither of us could understand a syllable. There were several of his priests and lawyers present (as I conjectured by their habits), who were commanded to address themselves to me; and I spoke to them in as many languages as I had the least smattering of, which were, High and Low Dutch, Latin, French, Spanish, Italian, and Lingua Franca;[15] but all to no purpose.

After about two hours the court retired, and I was left with a strong guard, to prevent the impertinence, and probably the malice of the rabble, who were very impatient to crowd about me as near as they durst; and some of them had the impudence to shoot their arrows at me, as I sat on the ground by the door of my house, whereof one very narrowly missed my left eye. But the colonel ordered six of the ring-leaders to be seized, and thought no punishment so proper as to deliver them bound into my hands; which some of his soldiers accordingly did, pushing them forwards with the butt-ends of their pikes into my reach. I took them all on my right hand, put five of them into my coat-pocket; and as to the sixth, I made a countenance as if I would eat him alive. The poor man squalled terribly, and the colonel and his officers were in much pain, especially when they saw me take out my penknife; but I soon put them out of fear, for, looking mildly, and immediately cutting the strings he was bound with, I set him gently on the ground, and away he ran. I treated the rest in the same manner, taking them one by one out of my pocket; and I observed both the soldiers and people were highly delighted at this mark of my clemency, which was represented very much to my advantage at court.

Towards night, I got with some difficulty into my house, where I lay on the ground, and continued to do so about a fortnight, during which time the emperor gave orders to have a bed prepared for me. Six hundred beds, of the common measure, were brought in carriages and worked up in my house; an hundred and fifty of their beds, sewn together, made up the breadth and length; and these were four double, which, however, kept me but very indifferently from the hardness of the floor, which was of smooth stone. By the same computation, they provided me with sheets, blankets, and coverlets, which were tolerable enough for one who had been so long inured to hardships as I.

As the news of my arrival spread through the kingdom, it brought prodigious numbers of rich, idle, and curious people to see me; so that the villages were almost emptied; and great neglect of tillage and household affairs must have ensued, if his imperial majesty had not provided, by several proclamations and orders of state, against this inconvenience. He directed that those who had already beheld me should return home, and not presume to come within fifty yards of my house without license from court; whereby the secretaries of state got considerable fees.

In the meantime, the emperor held frequent councils, to debate what course should be taken with me; and I was afterwards assured by a particular friend, a person of great quality, who was as much in the secret as any, that the court was under many difficulties concerning me. They apprehended my breaking loose; that my diet would be very expensive, and might cause a famine. Sometimes they determined to starve me, or at least to shoot me in the face and hands with poisoned arrows, which would soon despatch me: but again they considered that the stench of so large a carcase might produce a plague in the metropolis, and probably spread through the whole kingdom.

In the midst of these consultations, several officers of the army went to the door of the great council-chamber, and two of them being admitted, gave an account of my behavior to the six criminals above-mentioned, which made so favorable an impression in the breast of his majesty, and the whole board, in my behalf, that an imperial commission was issued out, obliging all the villages nine hundred yards round the city to deliver in, every morning, six beeves, forty sheep, and other victuals, for my sustenance; together with a proportionable quantity of bread and wine, and other liquors; for the due payment of which his majesty gave assignments upon his treasury. For this prince lives chiefly upon his own demesnes, seldom, except upon great occasions, raising any subsidies upon his subjects, who are bound to attend him in his wars at their own expense. An establishment was also made of six hundred persons, to be my domestics, who had board-wages allowed for their maintenance, and tents built for them very conveniently on each side of my door.

It was likewise ordered that three hundred tailors should make me a suit of clothes, after the fashion of the country; that six of his majesty's greatest scholars should be employed to instruct me in their language; and lastly, that the emperor's horses, and those of the nobility and troops of guards, should be frequently exercised in my sight, to accustom themselves to me.

All these orders were duly put in execution, and in about three weeks I made a great progress in learning their language; during which time the emperor frequently honored me with his visits, and was pleased to assist my masters in teaching me. We began already to converse together in some sort; and the first words I learnt were to express my desire that he would please give me my liberty, which I every day repeated on my knees. His answer, as I could apprehend it, was, that this must be a work of time, not to be thought on without the advice of his council, and that first I must *lumos kelmin pesso desmar lon emposo*; that is, swear a peace with him and his kingdom. However, that I should be used with all kindness; and he advised me to acquire, by my patience and discreet behavior, the good opinion of himself and his subjects.

He desired I would not take it ill, if he gave orders to certain proper officers to search me; for probably I might carry about me several weapons which must needs be dangerous things, if they answered the bulk of so prodigious a person. I said his majesty should be satisfied, for I was ready to strip myself and turn up my pockets before him. This I delivered, part in words, and part in signs.

He replied, that by the laws of the kingdom, I must be searched by two of his officers; that he knew this could not be done without my consent and assistance; that he had so good an opinion of my generosity and justice, as to trust their persons in my hands;

that whatever they took from me should be returned when I left the country, or paid for at the rate which I should set upon them. I took up the two officers in my hands, put them first into my coat-pockets, and then into every other pocket about me, except my two fobs and another secret pocket, which I had no mind should be searched, wherein I had some little necessaries that were of no consequence to any but myself. In one of

my fobs there was a silver watch, and in the other a small quantity of gold in a purse.

"THESE GENTLEMEN MADE AN EXACT INVENTORY OF EVERYTHING THEY SAW"

These gentlemen having pen, ink, and paper about them, made an exact inventory of everything they saw; and, when they had done, desired I would set them down, that they might deliver it to the emperor. This inventory I afterwards translated into English, and is word for word as follows:—

Imprimis,[16] In the right coat-pocket of the great man-mountain (for so I interpret the words *quinbus flestrin*), after the strictest search, we found only one great piece of coarse cloth, large enough to be a foot-cloth for your majesty's chief room of state. In the left pocket, we saw a huge silver chest, with a cover of the same metal, which we the searchers were not able to lift. We desired it should be opened, and one of us stepping into it, found himself up to the mid-leg in a sort of dust, some part whereof flying up to our faces, set us both a sneezing for several times together. In his right waistcoat pocket we found a prodigious number of white thin substances folded one over another, about the bigness of three men, tied with a strong cable, and marked with black figures; which we humbly conceive to be writings, every letter almost half as large as the palm of our hands. In the left, there was a sort of engine, from the back of which were extended twenty long poles, resembling the palisadoes before your majesty's court; wherewith we conjecture the man-mountain combs his head, for we did not always trouble him with questions, because we found it a great difficulty to make him understand us. In the large pocket on the right side of his middle cover (so I translate the word *ranfu-lo*, by which they meant my breeches), we saw a hollow pillar of iron, about the length of a man, fastened to a strong piece of timber, larger than the pillar; and upon one side of the pillar were huge pieces of iron sticking out, cut into strange figures, which we know not what to make of. In the left pocket, another engine of the same kind. In the smaller pocket on the right side were several round flat pieces of white and red metal, of different bulk; some of the white, which seemed to be silver, were so large and so heavy, that my comrade and I could hardly lift them. In the left pocket, were two black pillars irregularly shaped; we could not without difficulty reach the top of them, as we stood at the bottom of his pocket. One of them was covered, and seemed all of a piece; but at the upper end of the other, there appeared a white and round substance, about twice the bigness of our heads. Within each of these was enclosed a prodigious plate of steel, which, by our orders, we obliged him to show us, because we apprehended they might be dangerous engines. He took them out of their cases, and told us that in his own country his practice was to shave his beard with one of these, and to cut his meat with the other. There were two pockets which we could not enter: these he called his fobs. Out of the right fob hung a great silver chain, with a wonderful kind of engine at the bottom. We directed him to draw out whatever was at the end of that chain, which appeared to be a globe, half silver, and half of some transparent metal; for on the transparent side we saw certain strange figures, circularly drawn, and thought we could touch them till we found our fingers stopped by that lucid substance.[12] He put this engine to our ears, which made an incessant noise, like that of a water-mill; and we conjecture it is either some unknown animal, or the god that he worships; but we are more inclined to the latter opinion, because he assured us (if we understood him right, for he expressed himself very imperfectly), that he seldom did anything without consulting it. He called it his oracle, and said it pointed out the time for every action of his life. From the left fob he took out a net almost large enough for a fisherman, but contrived to open and shut like a purse, and served him for the same use; we found therein several massy pieces of yellow metal, which, if they be real gold, must be of immense value.

Having thus, in obedience to your majesty's commands, diligently searched all his pockets, we observed a girdle about his waist, made of the hide of some prodigious animal, from which, on the left side, hung a sword of the length of five men; and on the right, a bag or pouch, divided into two cells, each cell capable of holding three of your majesty's subjects. In one of these cells were several globes, or balls, of a most ponderous metal, about the bigness of our heads, and required a strong hand to lift them; the other cell contained a heap of certain black grains, but of no great bulk or weight, for we could hold about fifty of them in the palms of our hands.

This is an exact inventory of what we found about the body of the man-mountain, who used us with great civility and due respect to your majesty's commission. Signed and sealed, on the fourth day of the eighty-ninth moon of your majesty's auspicious reign.

CLEFRIN FRELOC.

MARSI FRELOC.

When this inventory was read over to the emperor, he directed me, although in very gentle terms, to deliver up the several particulars.

He first called for my scimitar, which I took out, scabbard and all. In the meantime, he ordered three thousand of his choicest troops (who then attended him) to surround me at a distance, with their bows and arrows just ready to discharge; but I did not observe it, for mine eyes were wholly fixed upon his majesty. He then desired me to draw my scimitar, which, although it had got some rust by the sea-water, was in most parts exceedingly bright. I did so, and immediately all the troops gave a shout between terror and surprise; for the sun shone clear, and the reflection dazzled their eyes, as I waved the scimitar to and fro in my hand. His majesty, who is a most magnanimous prince, was less daunted than I could expect; he ordered me to return it into the scabbard, and cast it on the ground as gently as I could, about six feet from the end of my chain.

The next thing he demanded was one of the hollow iron pillars, by which he meant my pocket-pistols. I drew it out, and at his desire, as well as I could, expressed to him the use of it; and charging it only with powder, which, by the closeness of my pouch, happened to escape wetting in the sea (an inconvenience against which all prudent mariners take special care to provide), I first cautioned the emperor not to be afraid, and then let it off in the air.

The astonishment here was much greater than at the sight of my scimitar. Hundreds fell down as if they had been struck dead; and even the emperor, although he stood his ground, could not recover himself in some time I delivered up both my pistols, in the same manner as I had done my scimitar, and then my pouch of powder and bullets, begging him that the former might be kept from fire, for it would kindle with the smallest spark, and blow up his imperial palace into the air.

I likewise delivered up my watch, which the emperor was very curious to see, and commanded two of his tallest yeomen of the guards[18] to bear it on a pole upon their shoulders, as draymen in England do a barrel of ale. He was amazed at the continual noise it made and the motion of the minute-hand, which he could easily discern; for their sight is much more acute than ours. He asked the opinions of his learned men about it, which were various and remote, as the reader may well imagine without my repeating; although, indeed, I could not very perfectly understand them.

I then gave up my silver and copper money, my purse, with nine large pieces of gold, and some smaller ones; my knife and razor, my comb and silver snuffbox, my handkerchief and journal-book. My scimitar, pistols, and pouch were conveyed in carriages to his majesty's stores; but the rest of my goods were returned to me.

I had, as I before observed, one private pocket, which escaped their search, wherein there was a pair of spectacles (which I sometimes use for the weakness of mine eyes), a pocket perspective,[19] and some other little conveniences; which, being of no consequence to the emperor, I did not think myself bound in honor to discover; and I apprehended they might be lost or spoiled if I ventured them out of my possession.

[12] *Stang:* an old word for a perch, sixteen feet and a half, also for a rood of ground.

[13] *Chairs:* a sedan chair is here meant. It held one person, and was carried by two men by means of projecting poles.

[14] *Crest:* a decoration to denote rank.

[15] *Lingua Franca:* a language—Italian mixed with Arabic, Greek, and Turkish—used by Frenchmen, Spaniards, and Italians trading with Arabs, Turks, and Greeks. It is the commercial language of Constantinople.

[16] *Imprimis:* in the first place, (pr.) im pri' mis.

[17] *Lucid:* shining, transparent.

[18] *Yeomen of the guards:* freemen forming the bodyguard of the sovereign.

[19] *Pocket perspective:* a small spy-glass or telescope.

CHAPTER III.

The Author Diverts the Emperor and His Nobility of Both Sexes in a Very Uncommon Manner. the Diversions of the Court of Lilliput Described. the Author Has His Liberty Granted Him Upon Certain Conditions.

My gentleness and good behavior had gained so far on the emperor and his court, and indeed upon the army and people in general, that I began to conceive hopes of getting my liberty in a short time, I took all possible methods to cultivate this favorable disposition. The natives came by degrees to be less apprehensive of any danger from me. I would sometimes lie down, and let five or six of them dance on my hand, and at last the boys and girls would venture to come and play at hide and seek in my hair. I had now made a good progress in understanding and speaking their language.

The emperor had a mind, one day, to entertain me with one of the country shows, wherein they exceed all nations I have known, both for dexterity and magnificence. I was diverted with none so much as that of the rope-dancers, performed upon a slender white thread, extended about two feet, and twelve inches from the ground. Upon which I shall desire liberty, with the reader's patience, to enlarge a little.

This diversion is only practised by those persons who are candidates for great employments and high favor at court. They are trained in this art from their youth, and are not always of noble birth or liberal education. When a great office is vacant, either by death or disgrace (which often happens) five or six of those candidates petition the emperor to entertain his majesty, and the court, with a dance on the rope, and whoever jumps the highest, without falling, succeeds in the office. Very often the chief ministers themselves are commanded to show their skill, and to convince the emperor that they have not lost their faculty. Flimnap, the treasurer, is allowed to cut a caper on the straight rope, at least an inch higher than any lord in the whole empire. I have seen him do the summersault several times together upon a trencher,[20] fixed on a rope, which is no thicker than a common packthread in England. My friend Reldresal, principal secretary for private affairs, is, in my opinion, if I am not partial, the second after the treasurer; the rest of the great officers are much upon a par.

These diversions are often attended with fatal accidents, whereof great numbers are on record. I myself have seen two or three candidates break a limb. But the danger is much greater when the ministers themselves are commanded to show their dexterity! for, by contending to excel themselves and their fellows, they strain so far that there is hardly one of them who hath not received a fall, and some of them two or three. I was assured that a year or two before my arrival, Flimnap would have infallibly broke his neck if one of the king's cushions, that accidentally lay on the ground, had not weakened the force of his fall.

There is likewise another diversion, which is only shown before the emperor and empress and first minister, upon particular occasions. The emperor lays on the table three fine silken threads, of six inches long; one is purple, the other yellow, and the third white. These threads are proposed as prizes for those persons whom the emperor hath a mind to distinguish by a peculiar mark of his favor. The ceremony is performed in his majesty's great chamber of state, where the candidates are to undergo a trial of dexterity very different from the former, and such as I have not observed the least resemblance of in any other country of the old or new world.

The emperor holds a stick in his hands, both ends parallel to the horizon, while the candidates, advancing one by one, sometimes leap over the stick, sometimes creep under it, backwards and forwards several times, according as the stick is advanced or depressed. Sometimes the emperor holds one end of the stick, and his first minister the other: sometimes the minister has it entirely to himself. Whoever performs his part with most agility, and holds out the longest in leaping and creeping, is rewarded with the blue-colored silk; the yellow is given to the next, and the green to the third, which they all wear girt twice about the middle; and you see few great persons round about this court who are not adorned with one of these girdles.

The horses of the army, and those of the royal stables, having been daily led before me, were no longer shy, but would come up to my very feet without starting. The riders would leap them over my hand as I held it on the ground; and one of the emperor's huntsmen, upon a large courser, took my foot, shoe and all, which was indeed a prodigious leap.

I had the good fortune to divert the emperor one day after a very extraordinary manner. I desired he would order several sticks of two feet high, and the thickness of an ordinary cane, to be brought me; whereupon his majesty commanded the master of his woods to give directions accordingly; and the next morning six wood-men arrived with as many carriages, drawn by eight horses to each.

I took nine of these sticks, and fixing them firmly in the ground in a quadrangular figure, two feet and a half square, I took four other sticks and tied them parallel at each corner, about two feet from the ground; then I fastened my handkerchief to the nine sticks that stood erect, and extended it on all sides, till it was as tight as the top of a drum; and the four parallel sticks, rising about five inches higher than the handkerchief, served as ledges on each side.

When I had finished my work, I desired the emperor to let a troop of his best horse, twenty-four in number, come and exercise upon this plain. His majesty approved of the proposal, and I took them up one by one in my hands, ready mounted and armed, with the proper officers to exercise them. As soon as they got into order, they divided into two parties, performed mock skirmishes, discharged blunt arrows, drew their swords, fled and pursued, attacked and retired, and, in short, discovered the best military discipline I ever beheld. The parallel sticks secured them and their horses from falling over the stage: and the emperor was so much delighted that he ordered this entertainment to be repeated several days, and once was pleased to be lifted up and give the word of command; and, with great difficulty, persuaded even the empress herself to let me hold her in her close chair within two yards of the stage, from whence she was able to take a full view of the whole performance.

It was my good fortune that no ill accident happened in these entertainments; only once a fiery horse, that belonged to one of the captains, pawing with his hoof, struck a hole in my handkerchief, and his foot slipping, he overthrew his rider and himself; but I immediately relieved them both, and covering the hole with one hand, I set down the troop with the other, in the same manner as I took them up. The horse that fell was strained in the left shoulder, but the rider got no hurt, and I repaired my handkerchief as well as I could; however, I would not trust to the strength of it any more in such dangerous enterprises.

About two or three days before I was set at liberty, as I was entertaining the court with feats of this kind, there arrived an express to inform his majesty that some of his subjects riding near the place where I was first taken up, had seen a great black substance lying on the ground, very oddly shaped, extending its edges round as wide as his majesty's bed-chamber, and rising up in the middle as high as a man; that it was no living creature, as they had at first apprehended, for it lay on the grass without motion; and some of them had walked round it several times; that, by mounting upon each other's shoulders, they had got to the top, which was flat and even, and, stamping upon it, they found it was hollow within; that they humbly conceived it might be something belonging to the man-mountain; and if his majesty pleased, they would undertake to bring it with only five horses.

I presently knew what they meant, and was glad at heart to receive this intelligence. It seems, upon my first reaching the shore after our shipwreck, I was in such confusion that, before I came to the place where I went to sleep, my hat, which I had fastened with a string to my head while I was rowing, and had stuck on all the time I was swimming, fell off after I came to land; the string, as I conjecture, breaking by some accident which I never observed, but thought my hat had been lost at sea. I intreated his imperial majesty to give orders it might be brought to me as soon as possible, describing to him the use and nature of it; and the next day the wagoners arrived with it, but not in a very good condition; they had bored two holes in the brim, within an inch and a half of the edge, and fastened two hooks in the holes; these hooks were tied by a long cord to the harness; and thus my hat was dragged along for above half an English mile; but the ground in that country being extremely smooth and level, it received less damage than I expected.

Two days after this adventure, the emperor, having ordered that part of the army which quarters in and about his metropolis to be in readiness, took a fancy of diverting himself in a very singular manner. He desired I would stand like a colossus, with my legs as far asunder as I conveniently could. He then commanded his general (who was an old, experienced leader and a great patron of mine) to draw up the troops in close order and march under me; the foot by twenty–four abreast and the horse by sixteen, with drums beating, colors flying, and pikes advanced. This body consisted of three thousand foot and a thousand horse.

I had sent so many memorials and petitions for my liberty, that his majesty at length mentioned the matter, first in the cabinet, and then in full council; where it was opposed by none, except Skyrris Bolgolam who was pleased, without any provocation, to be my mortal enemy. But it was carried against him by the whole board, and confirmed by the emperor. That minister was *galbet*, or admiral of the realm, very much in his master's confidence, and a person well versed in affairs, but of a morose and sour complexion. However, he was at length persuaded to comply; but prevailed, that the articles and conditions upon which I should be set free, and to which I must swear, should be drawn up by himself.

These articles were brought to me by Skyrris Bolgolam in person, attended by two under-secretaries, and several persons of distinction. After they were read, I was demanded to swear to the performance of them, first in the manner of my own country, and afterwards in the method prescribed by their laws; which was, to hold my right foot in my left hand, and to place the middle finger of my right hand on the crown of my head, and my thumb on the tip of my right ear.

But because the reader may be curious to have some idea of the style and manner of expression peculiar to that people, as well as to know the articles upon which I recovered my liberty, I have made a translation of the whole instrument, word for word, as near as I was able, which I here offer to the public.

Golbasto Momaren Evlame Gurdilo Shefin Mully Ully Gue, Most Mighty Emperor of Lilliput, delight and terror of the universe, whose dominions extend five thousand *blustrugs* (about twelve miles in circumference) to the extremities of the globe; monarch of all monarchs, taller than the sons of men; whose feet press down to the centre, and whose head strikes against the sun; at whose nod the princes of the earth shake their knees; pleasant as the spring, comfortable as the summer, fruitful as autumn, dreadful as winter. His most sublime majesty proposeth to the man-mountain, lately arrived at our celestial dominions, the following articles, which by a solemn oath he shall be obliged to perform.

First. The man-mountain shall not depart from our dominions without our license under our great seal.

Second. He shall not presume to come into our metropolis, without our express order, at which time the inhabitants shall have two hours warning to keep within doors.

Third. The said man-mountain shall confine his walks to our principal high roads, and not offer to walk or lie down in a meadow or field of corn.[21]

Fourth. As he walks the said roads, he shall take the utmost care not to trample upon the bodies of any of our loving subjects, their horses or carriages, nor take any of our subjects into his hands without their own consent.

Fifth. If an express requires extraordinary despatch, the man-mountain shall be obliged to carry in his pocket the messenger and horse a six-days' journey once in every moon, and return the said messenger back (if so required) safe to our imperial presence.

Sixth. He shall be our ally against our enemies in the island of Blefuscu, and do his utmost to destroy their fleet, which is now preparing to invade us.

Seventh. That the said man-mountain shall at his times of leisure be aiding and assisting to our workmen, in helping to raise certain great stones, towards covering the wall of the principal park, and other our royal buildings.

Eighth. That the said man-mountain shall, in two moons time, deliver in an exact survey of the circumference of our dominions, by a computation of his own paces round the coast.

Lastly. That upon his solemn oath to observe all the above articles, the said man-mountain shall have a daily allowance of meat and drink sufficient for the support of 1724 of our subjects, with free access to our royal person, and other marks of our favor. Given at our palace at Belfaborac, the twelfth day of the ninety-first moon of our reign.

I swore and subscribed to the articles with great cheerfulness and content, although some of them were not so honorable as I could have wished; which proceeded wholly from the malice of Skyrris Bolgolam, the high admiral; whereupon my chains were immediately unlocked, and I was at full liberty. The emperor himself in person did me the honor to be by at the whole ceremony. I made my acknowledgments, by prostrating myself at his majesty's feet: but he commanded me to rise; and after many gracious expressions, which, to avoid the censure of vanity, I shall not repeat, he added, that he hoped I should prove a useful servant, and well deserve all the favors he had already conferred upon me, or might do for the future.

The reader may please to observe, that, in the last article for the recovery of my liberty, the emperor stipulates to allow me a quantity of meat and drink sufficient for the support of 1724 Lilliputians. Some time after, asking a friend at court, how they came to fix on that determinate number, he told me, that his majesty's mathematicians having taken the height of my body by the help of a quadrant,[22] and finding it to exceed theirs in the proportion of twelve to one, they concluded, from the similarity of their bodies, that mine must contain at least 1724 of theirs, and consequently would require as much food as was necessary to support that number of Lilliputians. By which the reader may conceive an idea of the ingenuity of that people, as well as the prudent and exact economy of so great a prince.

---

[20] *Trencher:* a wooden plate or platter.

[21] *Corn:* such grains as wheat, rye, barley, oats.

[22] *Quadrant*: an instrument long used for measuring altitudes.

CHAPTER IV.

Milendo, the Metropolis of Lilliput, Described Together With the Emperor's Palace. a Conversation Between the Author and a Principal Secretary, Concerning the Affairs of That Empire. the Author Offers to Serve the Emperor in His Wars.

The first request I made, after I had obtained my liberty, was, that I might have license to see Milendo, the metropolis; which the emperor easily granted me, but with a special charge to do no hurt, either to the inhabitants or their houses. The people had notice, by proclamation, of my design to visit the town.

The wall, which encompassed it, is two feet and a half high, and at least eleven inches broad, so that a coach and horses may be driven very safely round it; and it is flanked with strong towers at ten feet distance. I stept over the great western gate, and passed very gently, and sideling, through the two principal streets, only in my short waistcoat, for fear of damaging the roofs and eaves of the houses with the skirts[23] of my coat. I walked with the utmost circumspection, to avoid treading on any stragglers who might remain in the streets; although the orders were very strict, that all people should keep in their houses at their own peril. The garret-windows and tops of houses were so crowded with spectators, that I thought in all my travels I had not seen a more populous place.

The city is an exact square, each side of the wall being five hundred feet long. The two great streets, which run across and divide it into four quarters, are five feet wide. The lanes and alleys, which I could not enter, but only viewed them as I passed, are from twelve to eighteen inches. The town is capable of holding five hundred thousand souls; the houses are from three to five stories; the shops and markets well provided.

The emperor's palace is in the centre of the city, where the two great streets meet. It is enclosed by a wall of two foot high, and twenty foot distant from the buildings. I had his majesty's permission to step over this wall; and the space being so wide between that and the palace, I could easily view it on every side.

The outward court is a square of forty feet, and includes two other courts; in the inmost are the royal apartments, which I was very desirous to see, but found it extremely difficult; for the great gates from one square into another were but eighteen inches high, and seven inches wide. Now the buildings of the outer court were at least five feet high, and it was impossible for me to stride over them without infinite damage to the pile, though the walls were strongly built of hewn stone, and four inches thick.

At the same time, the emperor had a great desire that I should see the magnificence of his palace; but this I was not able to do till three days after, which I spent in cutting down, with my knife, some of the largest trees in the royal park, about an hundred yards distance from the city. Of these trees I made two stools, each about three feet

high, and strong enough to bear my weight.

The people having received notice a second time, I went again through the city to the palace, with my two stools in my hands. When I came to the side of the outer court, I stood upon one stool, and took the other in my hand; this I lifted over the roof, and gently set it down on the space between the first and second court, which was eight feet wide. I then stept over the building very conveniently, from one stool to the other, and drew up the first after me with a hooked stick. By this contrivance I got into the inmost court; and, lying down upon my side, I applied my face to the windows of the middle stories, which were left open on purpose, and discovered the most splendid apartments that can be imagined. There I saw the empress and the young princes in their several lodgings, with their chief attendants about them. Her imperial majesty was pleased to smile very graciously upon me, and gave me out of the window her hand to kiss.

But I shall not anticipate the reader with farther descriptions of this kind, because I reserve them for a greater work, which is now almost ready for the press, containing a general description of this empire, from its first erection, through a long series of princes, with a particular account of their wars and politics, laws, learning, and religion, their plants and animals, their peculiar manners and customs, with other matters very curious and useful; my chief design, at present, being only to relate such events and transactions as happened to the public, or to myself, during a residence of about nine months in that empire.

One morning, about a fortnight after I had obtained my liberty, Reldresal, principal secretary (as they style him) for private affairs, came to my house, attended only by one servant. He ordered his coach to wait at a distance, and desired I would give him an hour's audience; which I readily consented to, on account of his quality and personal merits, as well as of the many good offices he had done me during my solicitations at court. I offered to lie down, that he might the more conveniently reach my ear; but he chose rather to let me hold him in my hand during our conversation.

He began with compliments on my liberty; said he might pretend to some merit in it. But however, added, that if it had not been for the present situation of things at court, perhaps I might not have obtained it so soon. For, said he, as flourishing a condition as we may appear to be in to foreigners, we labor under two mighty evils: a violent faction at home, and the danger of an invasion, by a most potent enemy, from abroad. As to the first, you are to understand, that, for above seventy moons past, there have been two struggling parties in this empire, under the names of *Tramecksan* and *Slamecksan*, from the high and low heels of their shoes, by which they distinguish themselves. It is alleged, indeed, that the high heels are most agreeable to our ancient constitution; but, however this may be, his majesty hath determined to make use only of low heels in the administration of the government, and all offices in the gift of the crown, as you cannot but observe: and particularly, that his majesty's imperial heels are lower, at least by a *drurr*, than any of his court (*drurr* is a measure about the fourteenth part of an inch). The animosities between these two parties run so high, that they will neither eat nor drink nor talk with each other. We compute the *Tramecksan*, or high heels, to exceed us in number; but the power is wholly on our side. We apprehend his imperial highness, the heir to the crown, to have some tendency towards the high heels; at least, we can plainly discover that one of his heels is higher than the other, which gives him a hobble in his gait. Now, in the midst of these intestine disquiets, we are threatened with an invasion from the island of Blefuscu, which is the other great empire of the universe, almost as large and powerful as this of his majesty. For, as to what we have heard you affirm, that there are other kingdoms and states in the world, inhabited by human creatures as large as yourself, our philosophers are in much doubt, and would rather conjecture that you dropped from the moon or one of the stars, because it is certain, that an hundred mortals of your bulk would, in a short time, destroy all the fruits and cattle of his majesty's dominions. Besides, our histories of six thousand moons make no mention of any other regions than the two great empires of Lilliput and Blefuscu. Which two mighty powers have, as I was going to tell you, been engaged in a most obstinate war for six-and-thirty moons past. It began upon the following occasion: It is allowed on all hands, that the primitive way of breaking eggs, before we eat them, was upon the larger end; but his present majesty's grandfather, while he was a boy, going to eat an egg, and breaking it according to the ancient practice, happened to cut one of his fingers. Whereupon the emperor, his father, published an edict, commanding all his subjects, upon great penalties, to break the smaller end of their eggs. The people so highly resented this law, that our histories tell us, there have been six rebellions raised on that account, wherein one emperor lost his life, and another his crown. These civil commotions were constantly fomented by the monarchs of Blefuscu; and when they were quelled, the exiles always fled for refuge to that empire. It is computed, that eleven thousand persons have, at several times, suffered death, rather than submit to break their eggs at the smaller end. Many hundred large volumes have been published upon this controversy, but the books of the Big-endians have been long forbidden, and the whole party rendered incapable, by law, of holding employments. During the course of these troubles, the Emperors of Blefuscu did frequently expostulate, by their ambassadors, accusing us of making a schism in religion, by offending against a fundamental doctrine of our great prophet Lustrog, in the fifty-fourth chapter of the Blundecral (which is their Alcoran)[24] This, however, is thought to be a mere strain upon the text; for the words are these: That all true believers break their eggs at the convenient end. And which is the convenient end, seems, in my humble opinion, to be left to every man's conscience, or, at least, in the power of the chief magistrate to determine. Now, the Big-endian exiles have found so much credit in the emperor of Blefuscu's court, and so much private assistance and encouragement from their party here at home, that a bloody war hath been carried on between the two empires for six-and-thirty moons, with various success; during which time we have lost forty capital ships, and a much greater number of smaller vessels, together with thirty thousand of our best seamen and soldiers; and the damage received by the enemy is reckoned to be somewhat greater than ours. However, they have now equipped a numerous fleet, and are just preparing to make a descent upon us; and his imperial majesty, placing great confidence in your valor and strength, hath commanded me to lay this account of his

affairs before you.

I desired the secretary to present my humble duty to the emperor, and to let him know that I thought it would not become me, who was a foreigner, to interfere with parties; but I was ready, with the hazard of my life, to defend his person and state against all invaders.

---

[23] *Skirt.* coat-tail.

[24] *Alcoran* the Koran or Mohammedan Bible.

CHAPTER V.

The Author, by an Extraordinary Stratagem, Prevents an Invasion. a High Title of Honor is Conferred Upon Him. Ambassadors Arrive From the Emperor of Blefuscu, and Sue for Peace. the Empress's Apartment on Fire, by Accident; the Author Instrumental in Saving the Rest of the Palace.

The empire of Blefuscu is an island, situate to the north northeast of Lilliput, from whence it is parted only by a channel of eight hundred yards wide. I had not yet seen it; and upon this notice of an intended invasion, I avoided appearing on that side of the coast, for fear of being discovered by some of the enemy's ships, who had received no intelligence of me, all intercourse between the two empires having been strictly forbidden during the war, upon the pain of death, and an embargo[25] laid by our emperor upon all vessels whatsoever.

I communicated to his majesty a project I had formed, of seizing the enemy's whole fleet; which, as our scouts assured us, lay at anchor in the harbor, ready to sail with the first fair wind. I consulted the most experienced seamen upon the depth of the channel, which they had often plumbed; who told me, that in the middle, at high water, it was seventy *glumgluffs* deep, which is about six feet of European measure; and the rest of it fifty *glumgluffs* at most. I walked towards the northeast coast, over against Blefuscu; where, lying down behind a hillock, I took out my small perspective glass, and viewed the enemy's fleet at anchor, consisting of about fifty men–of–war, and a great number of transports; I then came back to my house, and gave orders (for which I had a warrant) for a great quantity of the strongest cable and bars of iron. The cable was about as thick as packthread, and the bars of the length and size of a knitting needle. I trebled the cable, to make it stronger; and, for the same reason, I twisted three of the iron bars together, bending the extremities into a hook.

Having thus fixed fifty hooks to as many cables, I went back to the northeast coast, and putting off my coat, shoes, and stockings, walked into the sea in my leathern jerkin, about half an hour before high–water. I waded with what haste I could, and swam in the middle about thirty yards, till I felt ground; I arrived at the fleet in less than half an hour. The enemy were so frightened, when they saw me, that they leaped out of their ships, and swam to shore, where there could not be fewer than thirty thousand souls: I then took my tackling, and fastening a hook to the hole at the prow of each, I tied all the cords together at the end.

While I was thus employed, the enemy discharged several thousand arrows, many of which stuck in my hands and face; and, besides the excessive smart, gave me much disturbance in my work. My greatest apprehension was for mine eyes, which I should have infallibly lost, if I had not suddenly thought of an expedient. I kept, among other little necessaries, a pair of spectacles, in a private pocket, which, as I observed before, had escaped the emperor's searchers. These I took out, and fastened as strongly as I could upon my nose, and thus armed, went on boldly with my work, in spite of the enemy's arrows, many of which struck against the glasses of my spectacles, but without any other effect, farther than a little to discompose them.[26] I had now fastened all the hooks, and, taking the knot in my hand, began to pull: but not a ship would stir, for they were all too fast held by their anchors; so that the boldest part of my enterprise remained. I therefore let go the cord, and, leaving the hooks fixed to the ships, I resolutely cut with my knife the cables that fastened the anchors, receiving above two hundred shots in my face and hands; then I took up the knotted end of the cables, to which my hooks were tied, and, with great ease, drew fifty of the enemy's largest men-of-war after me.

The Blefuscudians, who had not the least imagination of what I intended, were at first confounded with astonishment. They had seen me cut the cables, and thought my design was only to let the ships run adrift, or fall foul on each other: but when they perceived the whole fleet moving in order, and saw me pulling at the end, they set up such a scream of grief and despair as it is almost impossible to describe or conceive. When I had got out of danger, I stopped awhile to pick out the arrows that stuck in my hands and face: and rubbed on some of the same ointment that was given me at my first arrival, as I have formerly mentioned. I then took off my spectacles, and waiting about an hour, till the tide was a little fallen, I waded through the middle with my cargo, and arrived safe at the royal port of Lilliput.

The emperor and his whole court stood on the shore, expecting the issue of this great adventure. They saw the ships move forward in a large half-moon, but could not discern me, who was up to my breast in water. When I advanced to the middle of the channel, they were yet more in pain, because I was under water to my neck. The emperor concluded me to be drowned, and that the enemy's fleet was approaching in an hostile manner: but he was soon eased of his fears; for the channel growing shallower every step I made, I came in a short time within hearing; and holding up the end of the cable, by which the fleet was fastened, I cried in a loud voice, Long live the most puissant[27] emperor of Lilliput! This great prince received me at my landing, with all possible encomiums, and created me a *nardac* upon the spot, which is the highest title of honor among them.

His majesty desired I would take some other opportunity of bringing all the rest of his enemy's ships into his ports. And so immeasurable is the ambition of princes, that he seemed to think of nothing less than reducing the whole empire of Blefuscu into a province, and governing it by viceroy; of destroying the Big-endian exiles, and compelling that people to break the smaller end of their eggs, by which he would remain the sole monarch of the whole world. But I endeavored to divert him from this design, by many arguments, drawn from the topics of policy, as well as justice. And I plainly protested, that I would never be an instrument of bringing a free and brave people into slavery. And when the matter was debated in council, the wisest part of the

ministry were of my opinion.

"AND CREATED ME A NARDAC UPON THE SPOT."

This open, bold declaration of mine was so opposite to the schemes and politics of his imperial majesty, that he could never forgive me; he mentioned it, in a very artful manner, at council, where, I was told, that some of the wisest appeared, at least by their silence, to be of my opinion; but others, who were my secret enemies, could not forbear some expressions, which by a side-wind reflected on me. And, from this time began an intrigue between his majesty and a junto[28] of ministers maliciously bent against me, which broke out in less than two months, and had like to have ended in my utter destruction. Of so little weight are the greatest services to princes, when put into the balance with a refusal to gratify their passions.

About three weeks after this exploit, there arrived a solemn embassy from Blefuscu, with humble offers of peace; which was soon concluded, upon conditions very advantageous to our emperor, wherewith I shall not trouble the reader. There were six ambassadors, with a train of about five hundred persons; and their entry was very magnificent, suitable to the grandeur of their master, and the importance of their business. When their treaty was finished, wherein I did them several good offices, by the credit I now had, or at least appeared to have at court, their excellencies, who were privately told how much I had been their friend, made me a visit in form. They began with many compliments upon my valor and generosity, invited me to that kingdom, in the emperor their master's name, and desired me to show some proofs of my prodigious strength, of which they had heard so many wonders; wherein I readily

obliged them, but shall not trouble the reader with the particulars.

When I had for some time entertained their Excellencies, to their infinite satisfaction and surprise, I desired they would do me the honor to present my most humble respects to the emperor their master, the renown of whose virtues had so justly filled the whole world with admiration, and whose royal person I resolved to attend, before I returned to my own country. Accordingly, the next time I had the honor to see our emperor, I desired his general license to wait on the Blefuscudian monarch, which he was pleased to grant me, as I could plainly perceive, in a very cold manner; but could not guess the reason, till I had a whisper from a certain person, that Flimnap and Bolgolam had represented my intercourse with those ambassadors as a mark of disaffection, from which, I am sure, my heart was wholly free. And this was the first time I began to conceive some imperfect idea of courts and ministers.

It is to be observed, that these ambassadors spoke to me by an interpreter, the languages of both empires differing as much from each other as any two in Europe, and each nation priding itself upon the antiquity, beauty, and energy of its own tongue, with an avowed contempt for that of its neighbor; yet our emperor, standing upon the advantage he had got by the seizure of their fleet, obliged them to deliver their credentials, and make their speech in the Lilliputian tongue.

And it must be confessed, that, from the great intercourse of trade and commerce between both realms; from the continual reception of exiles, which is mutual among them; and from the custom in each empire, to send their young nobility, and richer gentry, to the other, in order to polish themselves, by seeing the world, and understanding men and manners; there are few persons of distinction, or merchants, or, seamen, who dwell in the maritime parts, but what can hold conversation in both tongues, as I found some weeks after, when I went to pay my respects to the Emperor of Blefuscu, which, in the midst of great misfortunes, through the malice of my enemies, proved a very happy adventure to me, as I shall relate in its proper place.

The reader may remember, that when I signed those articles, upon which I recovered my liberty, there were some which I disliked, upon account of their being too servile; neither could anything but an extreme necessity have forced me to submit. But, being now a *nardac* of the highest rank in that empire, such offices were looked upon as below my dignity, and the emperor, to do him justice, never once mentioned them to me. However, it was not long before I had an opportunity of doing his majesty, at least as I then thought, a most signal service. I was alarmed at midnight with the cries of many hundred people at my door, by which, being suddenly awaked, I was in some kind of terror. I heard the word *burglum* repeated incessantly.

Several of the emperor's court, making their way through the crowd, entreated me to come immediately to the palace, where her imperial majesty's apartment was on fire, by the carelessness of a maid of honor, who fell asleep while she was reading a romance. I got up in an instant; and orders being given to clear the way before me, and it being likewise a moonshine night, I made a shift to get to the palace, without trampling on any of the people. I found they had already applied ladders to the walls of the apartment, and were well provided with buckets, but the water was at some distance. These buckets were about the size of a large thimble, and the poor people supplied me with them as fast as they could; but the flame was so violent that they did little good. I might easily have stifled it with my coat, which I unfortunately left behind me for haste, and came away only in my leathern jerkin. The case seemed wholly desperate and deplorable, and this magnificent palace would have infallibly been burnt down to the ground, if, by a presence of mind unusual to me, I had not suddenly thought of an expedient by which in three minutes the fire was wholly extinguished, and the rest of that noble pile, which had cost so many ages in erecting, preserved from destruction.

It was now daylight, and I returned to my house, without waiting to congratulate with the emperor; because, although I had done a very eminent piece of service, yet I could not tell how his majesty might resent the manner by which I had performed it: for, by the fundamental laws of the realm, it is capital in any man, of what quality soever, to even touch the empress or the royal princesses without invitation. But I was a little comforted by a message from his majesty, that he would give orders to the grand justiciary for passing my pardon in form, which, however, I could not obtain. And I was privately assured that the empress, conceiving the greatest abhorrence of me, and, in the presence of her chief confidants, could not forbear vowing revenge.

---

[25] *Embargo:* an order not to sail.

[26] *Discompose them:* displace them.

[27] *Puissant:* powerful.

[28] *Junto:* a body of men secretly united to gain some political end.

CHAPTER VI.

Of the Inhabitants of Lilliput; Their Learning, Laws, and Customs; the Manner of Educating Their Children. the Author's Way of Living in That Country.

Although I intend to leave the description of this empire to a particular treatise, yet, in the meantime, I am content to gratify the curious reader with some general ideas. As the common size of the natives is somewhat under six inches high, so there is an exact proportion in all other animals, as well as plants and trees: for instance, the tallest horses and oxen are between four and five inches in height, the sheep an inch and a half, more or less; their geese about the bigness of a sparrow, and so the several gradations downwards, till you come to the smallest, which, to my sight, were almost invisible; but nature hath adapted the eyes of the Lilliputians to all objects proper for their view; they see with great exactness, but at no great distance. And, to show the sharpness of their sight, towards objects that are near, I have been much pleased with observing a cook pulling[29] a lark, which was not so large as a common fly; and a young girl threading an invisible needle with invisible silk.

Their tallest trees are about seven feet high; I mean some of those in the great royal park, the tops whereof I could but just reach with my fist clenched. The other vegetables are in the same proportion; but this I leave to the reader's imagination.

I shall say but little at present of their learning, which, for many ages, hath flourished in all its branches among them: but their manner of writing is very peculiar, being neither from the left to the right like the Europeans; nor from the right to the left, like the Arabians; nor from up to down, like the Chinese, but aslant, from one corner of the paper to the other, like ladies in England.

They bury their dead with their heads directly downwards, because they hold an opinion, that in eleven thousand moons they are all to rise again, in which period the earth (which they conceive to be flat) will turn upside down, and by this means they shall, at the resurrection, be found ready, standing on their feet. The learned among them confess the absurdity of this doctrine, but the practice still continues, in compliance to the vulgar.

There are some laws and customs in this empire very peculiar; and, if they were not so directly contrary to those of my own dear country, I should be tempted to say a little in their justification. It is only to be wished they were as well executed. The first I shall mention relates to informers. All crimes against the state are punished here with the utmost severity; but, if the person accused maketh his innocence plainly to appear upon his trial, the accuser is immediately put to an ignominious death; and, out of his goods, or lands, the innocent person is quadruply recompensed for the loss of his time, for the danger he underwent, for the hardship of his imprisonment, and for all the charges he hath been at in making his defence, or, it that fund be deficient, it is largely supplied by the crown. The emperor also confers on him some public mark of his favor, and proclamation is made of his innocence through the whole city.

They look upon fraud as a greater crime than theft, and therefore seldom fail to punish it with death; for they allege, that care and vigilance, with a very common understanding, may preserve a man's goods from thieves, but honesty has no fence against superior cunning; and, since it is necessary that there should be a perpetual intercourse of buying and selling, and dealing upon credit, where fraud is permitted and connived at, or hath no law to punish it, the honest dealer is always undone, and the knave gets the advantage. I remember, when I was once interceding with the king for a criminal, who had wronged his master of a great sum of money, which he had received by order, and run away with, and happening to tell his majesty, by way of extenuation, that it was only a breach of trust, the emperor thought it monstrous in me, to offer as a defence the greatest aggravation of the crime; and, truly, I had little to say in return, farther than the common answer, that different nations had different customs; for, I confess, I was heartily ashamed.

Although we usually call reward and punishment the two hinges upon which all government turns, yet I could never observe this maxim to be put in practice by any nation except that of Lilliput. Whoever can there bring sufficient proof that he hath strictly observed the laws of his country for seventy-three moons, hath a claim to certain privileges, according to his quality and condition of life, with a proportionable sum of out of a fund appropriated for that use; he likewise acquires the title of *snillpall*, or *legal*, which is added to his name, but doth not descend to his posterity. And these people thought it a prodigious defect of policy among us, when I told them that our laws were enforced only by penalties, without any mention of reward. It is upon this account that the image of Justice, in their courts of judicature, is formed with six eyes, two before, as many behind, and on each side one, to signify circumspection, with a bag of gold open in her right hand, and a sword sheath in her left, to show she was more disposed to reward than to punish.

In choosing persons for all employments, they have more regard to good morals than to great abilities; for, since government is necessary to mankind, they believe that the common size of human understanding is fitted to some station or other, and that Providence never intended to make the management of public affairs a mystery, to be comprehended only by a few persons of sublime genius, of which there seldom are three born in an age; but they suppose truth, justice, temperance, and the like, to be in every man's power, the practice of which virtues, assisted by experience, and a good intention, would qualify any man for the service of his country, except where a course of study is required. But they thought the want of moral virtues was so far from being supplied by superior endowments of the mind, that employments could never be put into such dangerous hands as those of persons so qualified; and at least, that the mistakes committed by ignorance, in a virtuous disposition, would never be of such fatal consequences to the public weal as the practices of a man whose inclinations led him to be corrupt, and who had great abilities to manage, to multiply, and defend his corruptions.

In like manner, the disbelief of a Divine Providence renders a man incapable of holding any public station; for, since kings avow themselves to be the deputies of Providence, the Lilliputians think nothing can be more absurd than for a prince to employ such men as disown the authority under which he acts.

In relating these and the following laws, I would only be understood to mean the original institutions, and not the most scandalous corruptions into which these people are fallen, by the degenerate nature of man. For, as to that infamous practice of acquiring great employments by dancing on the ropes, or badges of favor and distinction by leaping over sticks, and creeping under them, the reader is to observe, that they were first introduced by the grandfather of the emperor, now reigning, and grew to the present height by the gradual increase of party and faction.

Ingratitude is, among them, a capital crime, as we read it to have been in some other countries; for they reason thus, that whoever makes ill returns to his benefactor, must needs be a common enemy to the rest of mankind, from whom he hath received no obligation, and therefore such a man is not fit to live.

Their notions relating to the duties of parents and children differ extremely from ours. Their opinion is, that parents are the last of all others to be trusted with the education of their own children; and, therefore, they have, in every town, public nurseries, where all parents, except cottagers and laborers, are obliged to send their infants of both sexes to be reared and educated, when they come to the age of twenty moons, at which time they are supposed to have some rudiments of docility. These schools are of several kinds, suited to different qualities, and to both sexes. They have certain professors, well skilled in preparing children for such a condition of life as befits the rank of their parents, and their own capacities as well as inclinations. I shall first say something of the male nurseries, and then of the female.

The nurseries for males of noble or eminent birth are provided with grave and learned professors, and their several deputies. The clothes and food of the children are plain and simple. They are bred up in the principles of honor, justice, courage, modesty, clemency, religion, and love of their country; they are always employed in some business, except in the times of eating and sleeping, which are very short, and two hours for diversions, consisting of bodily exercises. They are dressed by men till four years of age, and then are obliged to dress themselves, although their quality be ever so great; and the women attendants, who are aged proportionably to ours at fifty, perform only the most menial offices. They are never suffered to converse with servants, but go together in smaller or greater numbers to take their diversions, and always in the presence of a professor, or one of his deputies; whereby they avoid those early bad impressions of folly and vice, to which our children are subject. Their parents are suffered to see them only twice a year; the visit to last but an hour; they are allowed to kiss the child at meeting and parting; but a professor, who always stands by on those occasions, will not suffer them to whisper, or use any fondling expressions, or bring any presents of toys, sweetmeats, and the like.

The pension from each family, for the education and entertainment of a child, upon failure of due payment, is levied by the emperor's officers.

The nurseries for children of ordinary gentlemen, merchants, traders, and handicrafts, are managed proportionally after the same manner; only those designed for trades are put out apprentices at eleven years old, whereas those persons of quality continue in their exercises till fifteen, which answers to twenty-one with us; but the confinement is gradually lessened for the last three years.

In the female nurseries, the young girls of quality are educated much like the males, only they are dressed by orderly servants of their own sex; but always in the presence of a professor or deputy, till they come to dress themselves, which is at five years old. And if it be found that these nurses ever presume to entertain the girls with frightful or foolish stories, or the common follies practised by the chambermaids among us, they are publicly whipped thrice about the city, imprisoned for a year, and banished for life to the most desolate part of the country. Thus, the young ladies there are as much ashamed of being cowards and fools as the men, and despise all personal ornaments beyond decency and cleanliness: neither did I perceive any difference in their education, made by their difference of sex, only that the exercises of the women were not altogether so robust, and that some rules were given them relating to domestic life, and a smaller compass of learning was enjoined them: for their maxim is that, among people of quality, a wife should be always a reasonable and agreeable companion, because she cannot always be young. When the girls are twelve years old, which among them is the marriageable age, their parents or guardians take them home, with great expressions of gratitude to the professors, and seldom without tears of the young lady and her companions.

In the nurseries of females of the meaner sort, the children are instructed in all kinds of works proper for their sex and their several degrees; those intended for apprentices are dismissed at seven years old, the rest are kept to eleven.

The meaner[30] families who have children at these nurseries are obliged, besides their annual pension, which is as low as possible, to return to the steward of the nursery a small monthly share of their gettings, to be a portion[31] for the child; and, therefore, all parents are limited in their expenses by the law. For the Lilliputians think nothing can be more unjust than for people to leave the burden of supporting their children on the public. As to persons of quality, they give security to appropriate a certain sum for each child, suitable to their condition; and these funds are always managed with good husbandry and the most exact justice.

The cottagers and laborers keep their children at home, their business being only to till and cultivate the earth, and therefore their education is of little consequence to the public; but the old and diseased among them are supported by hospitals; for begging is a trade unknown in this empire.

And here it may perhaps divert the curious reader to give some account of my domestic,[32] and my manner of living in this country, during a residence of nine months and thirteen days. Having a head for mechanics, and being likewise forced by necessity, I had made for myself a table and chair, convenient enough, out of the largest trees in the royal park. Two hundred sempstresses were employed to make me shirts, and linen for my bed and table, all of the strongest and coarsest kind they could get; which, however, they were forced to quilt together in several folds, for the thickest was some degrees finer than lawn. Their linen is usually three inches wide, and three feet make a piece.

The sempstresses took my measure as I lay on the ground, one standing at my neck, and another at my mid-leg, with a strong cord extended that each held by the end, while a third measured the length of the cord with a rule of an inch long. Then they measured my right thumb, and desired no more; for, by a mathematical computation, that twice round the thumb is once round the wrist, and so on to the neck and the waist, and by the help of my old shirt, which I displayed on the ground before them for a pattern, they fitted me exactly. Three hundred tailors were employed in the same manner to make me clothes; but they had another contrivance for taking my measure. I kneeled down, and they raised a ladder from the ground to my neck; upon this ladder one of them mounted, and let fall a plumb-line from my collar to the floor, which just answered the length of my coat; but my waist and arms I measured myself. When my clothes were finished, which was done in my house (for the largest of theirs would not have been able to hold them), they looked like the patchwork made by the ladies in England, only that mine were all of a color.

I had three hundred cooks to dress my victuals, in little convenient huts built about my house, where they and their families lived, and prepared me two dishes a-piece. I took up twenty waiters in my hand, and placed them on the table; an hundred more attended below on the ground, some with dishes of meat, and some with barrels of wine and other liquors, flung on their shoulders; all of which the waiters above drew up, as I wanted, in a very ingenious manner, by certain cords, as we draw the bucket up a well in Europe. A dish of their meat was a good mouthful, and a barrel of their liquor a reasonable draught. Their mutton yields to ours, but their beef is excellent, I have had a sirloin so large that I have been forced to make three bites of it; but this is rare. My servants were astonished to see me eat it, bones and all, as in our country we do the leg of a lark. Their geese and turkeys I usually eat at a mouthful, and I must confess they far exceed ours. Of their smaller fowl, I could take up twenty or thirty at the end of my knife.

One day his imperial majesty, being informed of my way of living, desired that himself and his royal consort, with the young princes of the blood of both sexes, might have the happiness, as he was pleased to call it, of dining with me. They came accordingly, and I placed them in chairs of state upon my table, just over against me, with their guards about them. Flimnap, the lord high treasurer, attended there likewise, with his white staff; and I observed he often looked on me with a sour countenance, which I would not seem to regard, but eat more than usual, in honor to my dear country, as well as to fill the court with admiration. I have some private reasons to believe that this visit from his majesty gave Flimnap an opportunity of doing me ill offices to his master. That minister had always been my secret enemy, though he outwardly caressed me more than was usual to the moroseness of his nature. He represented to the emperor the low condition of his treasury; that he was forced to take up money at a great discount; that exchequer bills[33] would not circulate under nine per cent, below par; that I had cost his majesty above a million and a half of *sprugs* (their greatest gold coin, about the bigness of a spangle); and, upon the whole, that it would be advisable in

the emperor to take the first fair occasion of dismissing me.

"THE HAPPINESS ... OF DINING WITH ME."

46

[29] *Pulling:* plucking and drawing, preparatory to cooking,

[30] *Meaner:* of lower rank.

[31] *Portion:* the part of an estate given to a child.

[32] *Domestic:* the household and all pertaining thereto.

[33] *Exchequer bills:* bills of credit issued from the exchequer by authority of parliament.

CHAPTER VII.

The Author, Being Informed of a Design to Accuse Him of High Treason, Makes His Escape to Blefuscu. His Reception There.

Before I proceed to give an account of my leaving this kingdom, it may be proper to inform the reader of a private intrigue which had been for two months forming against me.

I had been hitherto all my life a stranger to courts, for which I was unqualified by the meanness of my condition. I had indeed heard and read enough of the dispositions of great princes and ministers, but never expected to have found such terrible effects of them in so remote a country, governed, as I thought, by very different maxims from those in Europe.

When I was just preparing to pay my attendance on the emperor of Blefuscu, a considerable person at court (to whom I had been very serviceable, at a time when he lay under the highest displeasure of his imperial majesty) came to my house very privately at night, in a close chair,[34] and without sending his name, desired admittance. The chairmen were dismissed; I put the chair, with his lordship in it, into my coat-pocket; and, giving orders to a trusty servant to say I was indisposed and gone to sleep, I fastened the door of my house, placed the chair on the table, according to my usual custom, and sat down by it. After the common salutations were over, observing his lordship's countenance full of concern, and inquiring into the reason, he desired I would hear him with patience, in a matter that highly concerned my honor and my life. His speech was to the following effect, for I took notes of it as soon as he left me:—

You are to know, said he, that several committees of council have been lately called in the most private manner on your account; and it is but two days since his majesty came to a full resolution.

You are very sensible that Skyrris Bolgolam (*galbet* or high-admiral) hath been your mortal enemy almost ever since your arrival: his original reasons I know not; but his hatred is increased since your great success against Blefuscu, by which his glory, as admiral, is much obscured. This lord, in conjunction with Flimnap the high treasurer, whose enmity against you is notorious, Limtoc the general, Lalcon the chamberlain, and Balmuff the grand justiciary, have prepared articles of impeachment against you, for treason, and other capital crimes.

This preface made me so impatient, being conscious of my own merits and innocence, that I was going to interrupt; when he entreated me to be silent, and thus proceeded.

"HE DESIRED I WOULD HEAR HIM WITH PATIENCE."

Out of gratitude for the favors you have done for me, I procured information of the whole proceedings, and a copy of the articles; wherein I venture my head for your service.

ARTICLES OF IMPEACHMENT AGAINST QUINBUS FLESTRIN, THE MAN-MOUNTAIN.

ARTICLE I.

Whereas, by a statute made in the reign of his Imperial Majesty Calin Deffar Plune, it is enacted, That whoever shall lay hands upon the empress, or upon any of the royal children, shall be liable to the pains and penalties of high treason. Notwithstanding, the said Quinbus Flestrin, in open breach of the said law, under color of extinguishing the fire kindled in the apartment of his Majesty's most dear imperial consort, did maliciously, and traitorously, pull her by the arms, and lift her high in the air in both his hands, against the statute in that case provided, etc., against the duty, etc.

ARTICLE II.

That the said Quinbus Flestrin, having brought the imperial fleet of Blefuscu into the royal port, and being afterwards commanded by his imperial majesty to seize all the other ships of the said empire of Blefuscu, and reduce that empire to a province, to be governed by a viceroy from hence, and to destroy and put to death, not only all the Big-endian exiles, but likewise all the people of that empire who would not immediately forsake the Big-endian heresy. He, the said Flestrin, like a false traitor against his most auspicious, serene, imperial majesty, did petition to be excused from the said service, upon pretence of unwillingness to force the consciences or destroy the liberties and lives of an innocent people.

ARTICLE III.

That, whereas certain ambassadors arrived from the court of Blefuscu, to sue for peace in his majesty's court; he, the said Flestrin, did, like a false traitor, aid, abet, comfort, and divert the said ambassadors, although he knew them to be servants to a prince who was lately an open enemy to his imperial majesty, and in open war against his said majesty.

ARTICLE IV.

That the said Quinbus Flestrin, contrary to the duty of a faithful subject, is now preparing to make a voyage to the court and empire of Blefuscu, for which he hath received only verbal license from his imperial majesty; and under color of the said license, doth falsely and traitorously intend to take the said voyage, and thereby to aid, comfort, and abet the emperor of Blefuscu, so late an enemy, and in open war with his imperial majesty aforesaid.

There are some other articles, but these are the most important, of which I have read you an abstract.

In the several debates upon this impeachment, it must be confessed that his majesty gave many marks of his great lenity, often urging the services you had done him, and endeavoring to extenuate your crimes. The treasurer and admiral insisted that you should be put to the most painful and ignominious death, by setting fire on your house at night; and the general was to attend, with twenty thousand men armed with poisoned arrows, to shoot you on the face and hands. Some of your servants were to have private orders to strew a poisonous juice on your shirts and sheets, which would soon make you tear your own flesh, and die in the utmost torture. The general came into the same opinion; so that for a long time there was a majority against you: but his majesty resolving, if possible, to spare your life, at last brought off the chamberlain.

Upon this incident, Reldresal, principal secretary for private affairs, who always approved himself your true friend, was commanded by the emperor to deliver his opinion, which he accordingly did; and therein justified the good thoughts you have of him. He allowed your crimes to be great, but that still there was room for mercy, the most commendable virtue in a prince, and for which his majesty was so justly celebrated. He said, the friendship between you and him was so well known to the world, that perhaps the most honorable board might think him partial; however, in obedience to the command he had received, he would freely offer his sentiments; that if his majesty, in consideration of your services, and pursuant to his own merciful disposition, would please to spare your life, and only give orders to put out both your eyes, he humbly conceived that, by this expedient, justice might in some measure be satisfied, and all the world would applaud the lenity of the emperor, as well as the fair and generous proceedings of those who have the honor to be his counsellors: that the loss of your eyes would be no impediment to your bodily strength, by which you might still be useful to his majesty: that blindness is an addition to courage, by concealing dangers from us: that the fear you had for your eyes was the greatest difficulty in bringing over the enemy's fleet: and it would be sufficient for you to see by the eyes of the ministers, since the greatest princes do no more.

This proposal was received with the utmost disapprobation by the whole board. Bolgolam, the admiral, could not preserve his temper, but rising up in fury, said he wondered how the secretary durst presume to give his opinion for preserving the life of a traitor: that the services you had performed were, by all true reasons of state, the great aggravation of your crimes: that you, who extinguished the fire in that unprincipled manner, might at another time inundate and drown the whole palace; and the same strength, which enabled you to bring over the enemy's fleet, might serve, upon the first discontent, to carry it back: that he had good reasons to think you were a Big-endian in your heart; and, as treason begins in the heart, before it appears in overt acts, so he accused you as a traitor on that account, and therefore insisted you should be put to death.

The treasurer was of the same opinion. He showed to what straits his majesty's revenue was reduced, by the charge of maintaining you, which would soon grow insupportable. That the secretary's expedient of putting out your eyes was so far from being a remedy against this evil, that it would probably increase it, as is manifest from the common practice of blinding some sort of fowls, after which they fed the faster, and grew sooner fat. That his sacred majesty, and the council, who are your judges, were to their own consciences fully convinced of your guilt, which was a sufficient argument to condemn you to death without the formal proofs required by the strict letter of the law.

But his imperial majesty, fully determined against capital punishment, was graciously pleaded to say, that since the council thought the loss of your eyes too easy a censure, some other might be inflicted hereafter. And your friend, the secretary, humbly desiring to be heard again, in answer to what the treasurer had objected concerning the great charge his majesty was at in maintaining you, said that his excellency, who had the sole disposal of the emperor's revenue, might easily provide against that evil, by gradually lessening your establishment; by which, for want of sufficient food, you would grow weak and faint, and lose your appetite, and consume in a few months; neither would the stench of your carcase be then so dangerous when it should become more than half diminished; and, immediately upon your death, five or six thousand of his majesty's subjects might in two or three days cut your flesh from your bones, take it away by cart-loads, and bury it in distant parts, to prevent infection, leaving the skeleton as a monument of admiration to posterity.

Thus, by the great friendship of the secretary, the whole affair was compromised. It was strictly enjoined that the project of starving you by degrees should be kept a secret, but the sentence of putting out your eyes was entered on the books, none dissenting except Bolgolam, the admiral, who, being a creature of the empress, was perpetually instigated by her majesty to insist upon your death, she having borne perpetual malice against you, on account of that illegal method you took to remove her and her children the night of the fire.

In three days, your friend the secretary will be directed to come to your house and read before you the articles of impeachment; and then to signify the great lenity and favor of his majesty and council, whereby you are only condemned to the loss of your eyes, which his majesty doth not question you will gratefully and humbly submit to; and twenty of his majesty's surgeons will attend, in order to see the operation well performed, by discharging very sharp-pointed arrows into the balls of your eyes as you lie on the ground.

I leave to your prudence what measures you will take; and, to avoid suspicion, I must immediately return, in as private a manner as I came.

His lordship did so, and I remained alone, under many doubts and perplexities of mind.

It was a custom, introduced by this prince and his ministry (very different, as I have been assured, from the practices of former times), that after the court had decreed any cruel execution either to gratify the monarch's resentment or the malice of a favorite, the emperor always made a speech to his whole council, expressing his great lenity and tenderness, as qualities known and confessed by all the world. This speech was immediately published through the kingdom; nor did anything terrify the people so much as those encomiums on his majesty's mercy; because it was observed that, the more these praises were enlarged and insisted on, the more inhuman was the punishment, and the sufferer more innocent. Yet, as to myself, I must confess, having never been designed for a courtier, either by my birth or education, I was so ill a judge of things that I could not discover the lenity and favor of this sentence, but conceived it (perhaps erroneously) rather to be rigorous than gentle, I sometimes thought of standing my trial; for although I could not deny the facts alleged in the several articles, yet I hoped they would admit of some extenuation. But having in my life perused many state-trials, which I ever observed to terminate as the judges thought fit to direct, I durst not rely on so dangerous a decision, in so critical a juncture, and against such powerful enemies. Once I was strongly bent upon resistance, for, while I had liberty, the whole strength of that empire could hardly subdue me, and I might easily with stones pelt the metropolis to pieces; but I soon rejected that project with horror, by remembering the oath I had made to the emperor, the favors I received from him, and the high title of *nardac* he conferred upon me. Neither had I so soon learned the gratitude of courtiers as to persuade myself that his majesty's present seventies acquitted me of all past obligations.

At last I fixed upon a resolution, for which it is probable I may incur some censure, and not unjustly; for I confess I owe the preserving mine eyes, and consequently my liberty, to my own great rashness and want of experience; because if I had then known the nature of princes and ministers, which I have since observed in many other courts, and their methods of treating criminals less obnoxious than myself, I should with great alacrity and readiness have submitted to so easy a punishment. But, hurried on by the precipitancy of youth, and having his imperial majesty's license to pay my attendance upon the emperor of Blefuscu, I took this opportunity, before the three days were elapsed, to send a letter to my friend the secretary, signifying my resolution of setting out that morning for Blefuscu pursuant to the leave I had got; and, without waiting for an answer, I went to that side of the island where our fleet lay. I seized a large man-of-war, tied a cable to the prow, and lifting up the anchors, I stript myself, put my clothes (together with my coverlet, which I carried under my arm) into the vessel, and drawing it after me, between wading and swimming arrived at the royal port of Blefuscu, where the people had long expected me; they lent me two guides to direct me to the capital city, which is of the same name. I held them in my hands until I came within two hundred yards of the gate, and desired them to signify my arrival to one of the secretaries, and let him know I there waited his majesty's command. I had an answer in about an hour, that his majesty, attended by the royal family and great officers of the court, was coming out to receive me. I advanced a hundred yards. The emperor and his train alighted from their horses, the empress and ladies from their coaches, and I did not perceive they were in any fright or concern. I lay on the ground

to kiss his majesty's and the empress's hand.

I told his majesty that I was come, according to my promise, and with the license of the emperor, my master, to have the honor of seeing so mighty a monarch, and to offer him any service in my power consistent with my duty to my own prince, not mentioning a word of my disgrace, because I had hitherto no regular information of it, and might suppose myself wholly ignorant of any such design; neither could I reasonably conceive that the emperor would discover the secret while I was out of his power, wherein however it soon appeared I was deceived.

I shall not trouble the reader with the particular account of my reception at this court, which was suitable to the generosity of so great a prince; nor of the difficulties I was in for want of a house and bed, being forced to lie on the ground, wrapped up in my coverlet.

CHAPTER VIII.

The Author, by a Lucky Accident, Finds Means to Leave Blefuscu, and After Some Difficulties, Returns Safe to His Native Country.

Three days after my arrival, walking out of curiosity to the northeast coast of the island, I observed, about half a league off in the sea, somewhat that looked like a boat overturned. I pulled off my shoes and stockings, and wading two or three hundred yards, I found the object to approach nearer by force of the tide; and then plainly saw it to be a real boat, which I supposed might by some tempest have been driven from a ship: whereupon I returned immediately towards the city, and desired his imperial majesty to lend me twenty of the tallest vessels he had left after the loss of his fleet, and three thousand seamen under the command of his vice-admiral. This fleet sailed round, while I went back the shortest way to the coast, where I first discovered the boat. I found the tide had driven it still nearer. The seamen were all provided with cordage, which I had beforehand twisted to a sufficient strength. When the ships came up, I stripped myself, and waded till I came within a hundred yards of the boat, after which I was forced to swim till I got up to it. The seamen threw me the end of the cord, which I fastened to a hole in the forepart of the boat, and the other end to a man-of-war. But I found all my labor to little purpose; for, being out of my depth, I was not able to work. In this necessity, I was forced to swim behind, and push the boat forwards as often as I could with one of my hands, and, the tide favoring me, I advanced so far, that I could just hold up my chin and feel the ground. I rested two or three minutes, and then gave the boat another shove, and so on till the sea was no higher than my arm-pits; and now, the most laborious part being over, I took out my other cables, which were stowed in one of the ships, and fastened them first to the boat, and then to nine of the vessels which attended me; the wind being favorable, the seamen towed, and I shoved, till we arrived within forty yards of the shore, and waiting till the tide was out, I got dry to the boat, and, by the assistance of two thousand men, with ropes and engines, I made a shift to turn it on its bottom, and found it was but little damaged.

I shall not trouble the reader with the difficulties I was under, by the help of certain paddles, which cost me ten days making, to get my boat to the royal port of Blefuscu, where a mighty concourse of people appeared upon my arrival, full of wonder at the sight of so prodigious a vessel. I told the emperor that my good fortune had thrown this boat in my way, to carry me to some place from whence I might return into my native country, and begged his majesty's orders for getting materials to fit it up, together with his license to depart, which, after some kind expostulation, he was pleased to grant.

I did very much wonder, in all this time, not to have heard of any express relating to me from our emperor to the court of Blefuscu. But I was afterwards given privately to understand that his imperial majesty, never imagining I had the least notice of his designs, believed I was only gone to Blefuscu in performance of my promise according to the license he had given me, which was well known at our court, and would return in a few days when the ceremony was ended. But he was at last in pain at my long absence; and, after consulting with the treasurer and the rest of that cabal,[25] a person of quality was despatched with the copy of the articles against me. This envoy had instructions to represent to the monarch of Blefuscu the great lenity of his master, who was content to punish me no farther than the loss of mine eyes; that I had fled from justice, and, if I did not return in two hours, I should be deprived of my title of *nardac* and declared a traitor. The envoy farther added that, in order to maintain the peace and amity between both empires, his master expected that his brother of Blefuscu would give orders to have me sent back to Lilliput, bound hand and foot, to be punished as a traitor.

The emperor of Blefuscu, having taken three days to consult, returned an answer consisting of many civilities and excuses. He said that, as for sending me bound, his brother knew it was impossible. That, although I had deprived him of his fleet, yet he owed great obligations to me for many good offices I had done him in making the peace. That, however, both their majesties would soon be made easy; for I had found a prodigious vessel on the shore, able to carry me on the sea, which he had given orders to fit up with my own assistance and direction; and he hoped in a few weeks both empires would be freed from so insupportable an incumbrance.

With this answer the envoy returned to Lilliput, and the monarch of Blefuscu related to me all that had passed; offering me at the same time (but under the strictest confidence) his gracious protection if I would continue in his service; wherein, although I believed him sincere, yet I resolved never more to put any confidence in princes or ministers where I could possibly avoid it; and, therefore, with all due acknowledgments for his favorable intentions, I humbly begged to be excused. I told him that, since fortune, whether good or evil, had thrown a vessel in my way, I was resolved to venture myself in the ocean, rather than be an occasion of difference between two such mighty monarchs. Neither did I find the emperor at all displeased; and I discovered, by a certain accident, that he was very glad of my resolution, and so were most of his ministers.

These considerations moved me to hasten my departure somewhat sooner than I intended; to which the court, impatient to have me gone, very readily contributed. Five hundred workmen were employed to make two sails to my boat, according to my directions, by quilting thirteen folds of their strongest linen together. I was at the pains of making ropes and cables, by twisting ten, twenty, or thirty of the thickest and strongest of theirs. A great stone, that I happened to find after a long search by the sea-shore, served me for an anchor. I had the tallow of three hundred cows for greasing my boat, and other uses. I was at incredible pains in cutting down some of the largest timber-trees for oars and masts, wherein I was, however, much assisted by his majesty's ship-carpenters, who helped me in smoothing them after I had done the rough work.

In about a month, when all was prepared, I sent to receive his majesty's commands, and to take my leave. The emperor and royal family came out of the palace. I lay down on my face to kiss his hand, which he very graciously gave me; so did the empress and young princes of the blood. His majesty presented me with fifty purses of two hundred *sprugs* a-piece, together with his picture at full length, which I put immediately into one of my gloves, to keep it from being hurt. The ceremonies at my departure were too many to trouble the reader with at this time.

"I SET SAIL AT SIX IN THE MORNING"

I stored the boat with the carcases of a hundred oxen, and three hundred sheep, with bread and drink proportionable, and as much meat ready dressed as four hundred cooks could provide. I took with me six cows and two bulls alive, with as many ewes and lambs, intending to carry them into my own country, and propagate the breed. And to feed them on board, I had a good bundle of hay and a bag of corn. I would gladly have taken a dozen of the natives, but this was a thing the emperor would by no means permit; and, besides a diligent search into my pockets, his majesty engaged my honor not to carry away any of his subjects, although with their own consent and desire.

Having thus prepared all things as well as I was able, I set sail on the twenty-fourth day of September, 1701, at six in the morning; and, when I had gone about four leagues to the northward, the wind being at southeast, at six in the evening I descried a small island about half a league to the northwest I advanced forward, and cast anchor on the lee side[34] of the island, which seemed to be uninhabited. I then took some refreshment, and went to my rest. I slept well, and, as I conjecture, at least six hours, for I found the day broke two hours after I awaked. It was a clear night. I ate my breakfast before the sun was up; and heaving anchor, the wind being favorable, I steered the same course that I had done the day before, wherein I was directed by my pocket-compass. My intention was to reach, if possible, one of those islands, which, I had reason to believe, lay to the northeast of Van Diemen's Land. I discovered nothing all that day; but upon the next, about three o'clock in the afternoon, when I had, by my computation, made twenty-four leagues from Blefuscu, I descried a sail steering to the southeast: my course was due east. I hailed her, but could get no answer; yet I found I gained upon her, for the wind slackened. I made all the sail I could, and in half-an-hour she spied me, then hung out her ancient,[37] and discharged a gun.

It is not easy to express the joy I was in, upon the unexpected hope of once more seeing my beloved country, and the dear pledges I left in it. The ship slackened her sails, and I came up with her, between five and six in the evening, September twenty-sixth; but my heart leaped within me to see her English colors. I put my cows and sheep into my coat-pockets, and got on board with all my little cargo of provisions. The vessel was an English merchantman returning from Japan by the North and South Seas; the captain, Mr. John Biddle, of Deptford, a very civil man and an excellent sailor. We were now in the latitude of 30 degrees south. There were about fifty men in the ship; and here I met an old comrade of mine, one Peter Williams, who gave me a good character to the captain. This gentleman treated me with kindness, and desired I would let him know what place I came from last, and whither I was bound; which I did in few words, but he thought I was raving, and that the dangers I had underwent had disturbed my head; whereupon I took my black cattle and sheep out of my pocket, which, after great astonishment, clearly convinced him of my veracity. I then showed him the gold given me by the emperor of Blefuscu, together with his majesty's picture at full length, and some other rareties of that country. I gave him two purses of two hundred *sprugs* each, and promised, when we arrived in England, to make him a present of a cow and a sheep.

I shall not trouble the reader with a particular account of this voyage, which was very prosperous for the most part. We arrived in the Downs[38] on the thirteenth of April, 1702. I had only one misfortune, that the rats on board carried away one of my sheep; I found her bones in a hole, picked clean from the flesh. I got the rest of my cattle safe ashore, and set them a-grazing in a bowling-green at Greenwich, where the fineness of the grass made them feed very heartily, though I had always feared the contrary: neither could I possibly have preserved them in so long a voyage, if the captain had not allowed me some of his best biscuits, which, rubbed to powder, and mingled with water, was their constant food. The short time I continued in England, I made a considerable profit by showing my cattle to many persons of quality and others: and before I began my second voyage I sold them for six hundred pounds.

Since my last return, I find the breed is considerably increased, especially the sheep, which I hope will prove much to the advantage of the woollen manufacture, by the fineness of the fleeces.

I stayed but two months with my wife and family; for my insatiable desire of seeing foreign countries would suffer me to continue no longer. I left fifteen hundred pounds with my wife and fixed her in a good house at Redriff. My remaining stock I carried with me, part in money, and part in goods, in hopes to improve my fortune. My eldest uncle, John, had left me an estate in land, near Epping, of about thirty pounds a year; and I had a long lease of the "Black Bull[39]," in Fetter Lane, which yielded me as much more: so that I was not in any danger of leaving my family upon the parish. My son Johnny, named so after his uncle, was at the grammar-school, and a towardly[40] child. My daughter Betty (who is now well married, and has children), was then at her needlework. I took leave of my wife and boy and girl, with tears on both sides, and went on board the "Adventure," a merchant ship of three hundred tons, bound for Surat, Captain John Nicholas, of Liverpool, commander. But my account of this voyage must be referred to the second part of my travels.

THE END OF THE FIRST PART.

"THEY CONCLUDED ... THAT I WAS ONLY Relplum Scalcath,"

---

[35] *Cabal:* a body of men united for some sinister purpose.

[36] *Lee side:* side sheltered from the wind.

[37] *Ancient:* flag, corrupted from ensign.

[38] *Downs:* A famous natural roadstead off the southeast coast of Kent, between Goodwin Sands and the mainland, south of the Thames entrance.

[39] *Black Bull:* inns in England are often named after animals with an adjective descriptive of the color of the sign; as, *The Golden Lion, The White Horse.*

[40] *Towardly:* apt, docile.

PART II: A VOYAGE TO BROBDINGNAG.

CHAPTER I.

A Great Storm Described; the Long-boat Sent to Fetch Water; the Author Goes With It to Discover the Country. He is Left on Shore, is Seized by One of the Natives, and Carried to a Farmer's House. His Reception, With Several Accidents That Happened There. a Description of the Inhabitants.

Having been condemned by nature and fortune to an active and restless life, in two months after my return I again left my native country, and took shipping in the Downs on the twentieth day of June, 1702, in the "Adventure," Captain John Nicholas, a Cornish man, commander, bound for Surat. We had a very prosperous gale till we arrived at the Cape of Good Hope, where we landed for fresh water; but, discovering a leak, we unshipped our goods and wintered there: for, the captain falling sick of an ague, we could not leave the Cape till the end of March. We then set sail, and had a good voyage till we passed the Straits of Madagascar;[41] but having got northward of that island, and to about five degrees south latitude, the winds, which in those seas are observed to blow a constant equal gale, between the north and west, from the beginning of December to the beginning of May, on the nineteenth of April began to blow with much greater violence and more westerly than usual, continuing so for twenty days together, during which time we were driven a little to the east of the Molucca Islands, and about three degrees northward of the line,[42] as our captain found by an observation he took the second of May, at which time the wind ceased and it was a perfect calm; whereat I was not a little rejoiced. But, he, being a man well experienced in the navigation of those seas, bid us all prepare against a storm, which accordingly happened the day following: for the southern wind, called the southern monsoon, began to set in, and soon it was a fierce storm.

Finding it was like to overblow, we took in our sprit–sail, and stood by to hand the foresail; but making foul weather, we looked the guns were all fast, and handed the mizzen.

map02.jpg

The ship lay very broad off, so we thought it better spooning before the sea, than trying, or hulling. We reefed the foresail and set him, we hauled aft the foresheet: the helm was hard-a-weather. The ship wore bravely. We belayed the fore down-haul; but the sail was split, and we hauled down the yard, and got the sail into the ship, and unbound all the things clear of it. It was a very fierce storm; the sea broke strange and dangerous. We hauled off the laniard of the whipstaff, and helped the man at the helm. We could not get down our topmast, but let all stand, because she scudded before the sea very well, and we knew that the topmast being aloft, the ship was the wholesomer, and made better way through the sea, seeing we had sea-room. When the storm was over, we set foresail and mainsail, and brought the ship to. Then we set the mizzen, main-top-sail, and the fore-top-sail. Our course was east north east, the wind was at southwest. We got the starboard tacks aboard, we cast off our weather braces and lifts; we set in the lee braces, and hauled forward by the weather bowlings, and hauled them tight and belayed them, and hauled over the mizzen tack to wind-ward and kept her full and by, as near as she could lie.

During this storm, which was followed by a strong wind, west southwest, we were carried, by my computation, about five hundred leagues to the east, so that the oldest sailor on board could not tell in what part of the world we were. Our provisions held out well, our ship was staunch, and our crew all in good health; but we lay in the utmost distress for water. We thought it best to hold on the same course, rather than turn more northerly, which might have brought us to the northwest parts of Great Tartary, and into the Frozen Sea.

On the sixteenth day of June, 1703, a boy on the topmast discovered land. On the seventeenth, we came in full view of a great island or continent (for we knew not which), on the south side whereof was a small neck of land, jutting out into the sea, and a creek too shallow to hold a ship of above one hundred tons. We cast anchor within a league of this creek, and our captain sent a dozen of his men well armed in the long-boat, with vessels for water, if any could be found. I desired his leave to go with them, that I might see the country, and make what discoveries I could.

When we came to land, we saw no river or spring, nor any sign of inhabitants. Our men therefore wandered on the shore to find out some fresh water near the sea, and I walked alone about a mile on the other side, where I observed the country all barren and rocky. I now began to be weary, and seeing nothing to entertain my curiosity, I returned gently down toward the creek; and the sea being full in my view, I saw our men already got into the boat, and rowing for life to the ship. I was going to holla after them, although it had been to little purpose, when I observed a huge creature walking after them in the sea, as fast as he could; he waded not much deeper than his knees, and took prodigious strides; but our men had the start of him about half a league, and the sea thereabouts being full of pointed rocks, the monster was not able to overtake the boat. This I was afterwards told, for I durst not stay to see the issue of the adventure; but ran as fast as I could the way I first went, and then climbed up a steep hill, which gave me some prospect of the country. I found it fully cultivated; but that which first surprised me was the length of the grass, which, in those grounds that seemed to be kept for hay, was about twenty feet high.

"A HUGE CREATURE WALKING ... IN THE SEA."

I fell into a high road, for so I took it to be, though it served to the inhabitants only as a footpath through a field of barley. Here I walked on for some time, but could see little on either side, it being now near harvest, and the corn rising at least forty feet. I was an hour walking to the end of this field, which was fenced in with a hedge of at least one hundred and twenty feet high, and the trees so lofty that I could make no computation of their altitude. There was a stile to pass from this field into the next. It had four steps, and a stone to cross over when you came to the uppermost. It was impossible for me to climb this stile because every step was six feet high, and the upper stone above twenty.

I was endeavoring to find some gap in the hedge, when I discovered one of the inhabitants in the next field, advancing towards the stile, of the same size with him whom I saw in the sea pursuing our boat. He appeared as tall as an ordinary spire steeple, and took about ten yards at every stride, as near as I could guess. I was struck with the utmost fear and astonishment, and ran to hide myself in the corn, from whence I saw him at the top of the stile, looking back into the next field on the right hand, and heard him call in a voice many degrees louder than a speaking trumpet; but the noise was so high in the air that at first I certainly thought it was thunder. Whereupon seven monsters, like himself, came towards him with reaping-hooks in their hands, each hook about the largeness of six scythes. These people were not so well clad as the first, whose servants or laborers they seemed to be; for, upon some words he spoke, they went to reap the corn in the field where I lay. I kept from them at as great a distance as I could, but was forced to move, with extreme difficulty, for the stalks of the corn were sometimes not above a foot distance, so that I could hardly squeeze my body betwixt them. However, I made a shift to go forward till I came to a part of the field where the corn had been laid by the rain and wind. Here it was impossible for me to advance a step; for the stalks were so interwoven that I could not creep through, and the beards of the fallen ears so strong and pointed that they pierced through my clothes into my flesh. At the same time I heard the reapers not above a hundred yards behind me.

Being quite dispirited with toil, and wholly overcome by grief and despair, I lay down between two ridges, and heartily wished I might there end my days. I bemoaned my desolate widow and fatherless children. I lamented my own folly and wilfulness in attempting a second voyage against the advice of all my friends and relations. In this terrible agitation of mind, I could not forbear thinking of Lilliput, whose inhabitants looked upon me as the greatest prodigy that ever appeared in the world; where I was able to draw an imperial fleet in my hand, and perform those other actions which will be recorded forever in the chronicles of that empire, while posterity shall hardly believe them, although attested by millions. I reflected what a mortification it must prove to me to appear as inconsiderable in this nation as one single Lilliputian would be among us. But this I conceived was to be among the least of my misfortunes: for, as human creatures are observed to be more savage and cruel in proportion to their bulk, what could I expect but to be a morsel in the mouth of the first among these enormous barbarians that should happen to seize me? Undoubtedly philosophers are in the right when they tell us that nothing is great or little otherwise than by comparison. It might have pleased fortune to let the Lilliputians find some nation where the people were as diminutive with respect to them as they were to me. And who knows but that even this prodigious race of mortals might be equally overmatched in some distant part of the world, whereof we have yet no discovery?

Scared and confounded as I was, I could not forbear going on with these reflections, when one of the reapers, approaching within ten yards of the ridge where I lay, made me apprehend that with the next step I should be squashed to death under his foot, or cut in two with his reaping–hook. And, therefore, when he was again about to move, I screamed as loud as fear could make me. Whereupon the huge creature trod short, and looking round about under him for some time, at last espied me as I lay on the ground. He considered awhile, with the caution of one who endeavors to lay hold on a small dangerous animal in such a manner that it shall not be able either to scratch or to bite him, as I myself have sometimes done with a weasel in England.

"WHEREUPON THE HUGE CREATURE TROD SHORT."

At length he ventured to take me up between his forefinger and thumb, and brought me within three yards of his eyes, that he might behold my shape more perfectly. I guessed his meaning, and my good fortune gave me so much presence of mind that I resolved not to struggle in the least as he held me in the air, above sixty feet from the ground, although he grievously pinched my sides, for fear I should slip through his fingers. All I ventured was to raise my eyes towards the sun, and place my hands together in a supplicating posture, and to speak some words in an humble melancholy tone, suitable to the condition I then was in. For I apprehended every moment that he would dash me against the ground, as we usually do any little hateful animal which we have a mind to destroy. But my good star would have it that he appeared pleased with my voice and gestures, and began to look upon me as a curiosity, much wondering to hear me pronounce articulate words, although he could not understand them. In the meantime I was not able to forbear groaning and shedding tears, and turning my head towards my sides; letting him know, as well as I could, how cruelly I was hurt by the pressure of his thumb and finger. He seemed to apprehend my meaning; for, lifting up the lappet of his coat, he put me gently into it, and immediately ran along with me to his master, who was a substantial farmer, and the same person I had first seen in the field.

The farmer, having (as I suppose by their talk) received such an account of me as his servant could give him, took a piece of a small straw, about the size of a walking-staff, and therewith lifted up the lappets of my coat, which it seems he thought to be some kind of covering that nature had given me. He blew my hair aside, to take a better view of my face. He called his hinds[43] about him, and asked them (as I afterwards learned) whether they had ever seen in the fields any little creature that resembled me. He then placed me softly on the ground upon all fours, but I got immediately up, and walked slowly backwards and forwards to let those people see that I had no intent to run away.

They all sat down in a circle about me, the better to observe my motions. I pulled off my hat, and made a low bow towards the farmer. I fell on my knees, and lifted up my hands and eyes, and spoke several words as loud as I could: I took a purse of gold out of my pocket, and humbly presented it to him. He received it on the palm of his hand, then applied it close to his eye to see what it was, and afterwards turned it several times with the point of a pin (which he took out of his sleeve), but could make nothing of it. Whereupon I made a sign that he should place his hand on the ground. I then took the purse, and opening it, poured all the gold into his palm. There were six Spanish pieces, of four pistoles[44] each, besides twenty or thirty smaller coins. I saw him wet the tip of his little finger upon his tongue, and take up one of my largest pieces, and then another, but he seemed to be wholly ignorant what they were. He made me a sign to put them again into my purse, and the purse again into my pocket, which, after offering it to him several times, I thought it best to do.

The farmer by this time was convinced I must be a rational creature. He spoke often to me, but the sound of his voice pierced my ears like that of a water-mill, yet his words were articulate enough. I answered as loud as I could in several languages, and he often laid his ear within two yards of me; but all in vain, for we were wholly unintelligible to each other. He then sent his servants to their work, and taking his handkerchief out of his pocket, he doubled and spread it on his left hand, which he placed flat on the ground, with the palm upwards, making me a sign to step into it, as I could easily do, for it was not above a foot in thickness.

I thought it my part to obey, and, for fear of falling, laid myself at full length upon the handkerchief, with the remainder of which he lapped me up to the head for farther security, and in this manner carried me home to his house. There he called his wife, and showed me to her; but she screamed and ran back, as women in England do at the sight of a toad or a spider. However, when she had awhile seen my behavior, and how well I observed the signs her husband made, she was soon reconciled, and by degrees grew extremely tender of me.

It was about twelve at noon, and a servant brought in dinner. It was only one substantial dish of meat (fit for the plain condition of an husbandman) in a dish of about four-and-twenty feet diameter. The company were the farmer and his wife, three children, and an old grandmother. When they were sat down, the farmer placed me at some distance from him on the table, which was thirty feet high from the floor. I was in a terrible fright, and kept as far as I could from the edge for fear of falling. The wife minced a bit of meat, then crumbled some bread on a trencher,[45] and placed it before me. I made her a low bow, took out my knife and fork, and fell to eat, which gave them exceeding delight.

The mistress sent her maid for a small dram cup, which held about three gallons, and filled it with drink: I took up the vessel with much difficulty in both hands, and in a most respectful manner drank to her ladyship's health, expressing the words as loud as I could in English, which made the company laugh so heartily that I was almost deafened by the noise. This liquor tasted like a small cider, and was not unpleasant. Then the master made me a sign to come to his trencher-side; but as I walked on the table, being in great surprise all the time, as the indulgent reader will easily conceive and excuse, I happened to stumble against a crust, and fell flat on my face, but received no hurt. I got up immediately, and observing the good people to be in much concern, I took my hat (which I held under my arm out of good manners), and, waving it over my head, made three huzzas, to show that I had got no mischief by my fall.

But advancing forwards towards my master (as I shall henceforth call him), his youngest son, who sat next him, an arch boy of about ten years old, took me up by the legs, and held me so high in the air, that I trembled in every limb; but his father snatched me from him, and at the same time gave him such a box in the left ear as would have felled an European troop of horse to the earth, ordering him to be taken from the table. But being afraid the boy might owe me a spite, and well remembering how mischievous all children among us naturally are to sparrows, rabbits, young kittens, and puppy dogs, I fell on my knees, and, pointing to the boy, made my master to understand as well as I could, that I desired his son might be pardoned. The father complied, and the lad took his seat again; whereupon I went to him and kissed his hand, which my master took, and made him stroke me gently with it.

70

In the midst of dinner, my mistress's favorite cat leapt into her lap. I heard a noise behind me like that of a dozen stocking-weavers at work; and, turning my head, I found it proceeded from the purring of that animal, who seemed to be three times larger than an ox, as I computed by the view of her head and one of her paws, while her mistress was feeding and stroking her. The fierceness of this creature's countenance altogether discomposed me, though I stood at the further end of the table, above fifty feet off, and although my mistress held her fast, for fear she might give a spring and seize me in her talons.

But it happened there was no danger; for the cat took not the least notice of me, when my master placed me within three yards of her. And as I have been always told, and found true by experience in my travels, that flying or discovering[46] fear before a fierce animal is a certain way to make it pursue or attack you, so I resolved in this dangerous juncture to show no manner of concern. I walked with intrepidity five or six times before the very head of the cat, and came within half a yard of her; whereupon she drew herself back, as if she were more afraid of me. I had less apprehension concerning the dogs, whereof three or four came into the room, as it is usual in farmers' houses; one of which was a mastiff equal in bulk to four elephants, and a greyhound somewhat taller than the mastiff, but not so large.

When dinner was almost done, the nurse came in with a child of a year old in her arms, who immediately spied me, and began a squall that you might have heard from London Bridge to Chelsea,[47] after the usual oratory of infants, to get me for a plaything. The mother out of pure indulgence took me up, and put me towards the child, who presently seized me by the middle and got my head in its mouth, where I roared so loud that the urchin was frighted, and let me drop, and I should infallibly have broke my neck if the mother had not held her apron under me. The nurse, to quiet her babe, made use of a rattle, which was a kind of hollow vessel filled with great stones, and fastened by a cable to the child's waist. As she sat down close to the table on which I stood, her appearance astonished me not a little. This made me reflect upon the fair skins of our English ladies, who appear so beautiful to us, only because they are of our own size, and their defects not to be seen but through a magnifying glass, where we find by experiment that the smoothest and whitest skins look rough, and coarse and ill-colored.

I remember, when I was at Lilliput, the complexions of those diminutive people appeared to me the fairest in the world; and talking upon this subject with a person of learning there, who was an intimate friend of mine, he said that my face appeared much fairer and smoother when he looked on me from the ground than it did upon a nearer view, when I took him up in my hand and brought him close, which he confessed was at first a very shocking sight. He said he could discover great holes in my skin; that the stumps of my beard were ten times stronger than the bristles of a boar, and my complexion made up of several colors altogether disagreeable: although I must beg leave to say for myself that I am as fair as most of my sex and country, and very little sunburnt by my travels. On the other side, discoursing of the ladies of that emperor's court, he used to tell me one had freckles, another too wide a mouth, a third too large a nose, nothing of which I was able to distinguish. I confess this reflection was obvious enough; which, however, I could not forbear, lest the reader might think those vast creatures were actually deformed: for I must do them justice to say they are a comely race of people; and particularly the features of my master's countenance, although he were but a farmer, when I beheld him from the height of sixty feet, appeared very well proportioned.

When dinner was done my master went out to his labors, and, as I could discover by his voice and gestures, gave his wife a strict charge to take care of me. I was very much tired and disposed to sleep, which, my mistress perceiving, she put me on her own bed, and covered me with a clean white handkerchief, but larger and coarser than the mainsail of a man-of-war.

I slept about two hours, and dreamed I was at home with my wife and children, which aggravated my sorrows when I awaked and found myself alone in a vast room, between two and three hundred feet wide, and above two hundred high, lying in a bed twenty yards wide. My mistress was gone about her household affairs, and had locked me in. The bed was eight yards from the floor.

"I ... DREW MY HANGER TO DEFEND MYSELF."

Presently two rats crept up the curtains, and ran smelling backwards and forwards on my bed. One of them came almost up to my face; whereupon I rose in a fright, and drew out my hanger to defend myself. The horrible animals had the boldness to attack me both sides, and one of them held his forefeet at my collar; but I killed him before he could do me any mischief. He fell down at my feet; and the other, seeing the fate of his comrade, made his escape, but not without one good wound on the back, which I gave him as he fled, and made the blood run trickling from him. After this exploit I walked gently to and fro on the bed to recover my breath and loss of spirits. These creatures were of the size of a large mastiff, but infinitely more nimble and fierce; so that, if I had taken off my belt before I went to sleep, I must infallibly have been torn to pieces and devoured. I measured the tail of the dead rat, and found it to be two yards long wanting an inch; but it went against my stomach to draw the carcase off the bed, where it still lay bleeding. I observed it had yet some life; but, with a strong slash across the neck, I thoroughly despatched it.

I hope the gentle reader will excuse me for dwelling on these and the like particulars, which, however insignificant they may appear to grovelling vulgar minds, yet will certainly help a philosopher to enlarge his thoughts and imagination, and apply them to the benefit of public as well as private life, which was my sole design in presenting this and other accounts of my travels to the world; wherein I have been chiefly studious of truth, without affecting any ornaments of teaming or style. But the whole scene of this voyage made so strong an impression on my mind, and is so deeply memory, that in committing it to paper I did not omit one material circumstance. However, upon a strict review, I blotted out several passages of less moment which were in my first copy, for fear of being censured as tedious and trifling, whereof travellers are often, perhaps not without justice, accused.

---

[41] *Straits of Madagascar*: Mozambique Channel.

[42] *The line*: the equator.

[43] *Hinds*: peasants; rustics.

[44] *Pistoles*: about three dollars and sixty cents.

[45] *Trencher-side*: up to his trencher or wooden plate.

[46] *Discovering*: Showing.

[47].*From London Bridge to Chelsea*: about three miles as the birds fly.

CHAPTER II.

A Description of the Farmer's Daughter. the Author Carried to a Market-town, and Then to the Metropolis. the Particulars of This Journey.

My mistress had a daughter of nine years old, a child of toward parts for her age, very dexterous at her needle, and skilful in dressing her baby. Her mother and she contrived to fit up the baby's cradle for me against night. The cradle was put into a small drawer cabinet, and the drawer placed upon a hanging shelf for fear of the rats. This was my bed all the time I stayed with these people, though made more convenient by degrees, as I began to learn their language and make my wants known.

She made me seven shirts, and some other linen, of as fine cloth as could be got, which indeed was coarser than sackcloth; and these she constantly washed for me with her own hands. She was likewise my school-mistress, to teach me the language. When I pointed to anything, she told me the name of it in her own tongue, so that in a few days I was able to call for whatever I had a mind to. She was very good-natured, and not above forty feet high, being little for her age. She gave me the name of Grildrig, which the family took up, and afterwards the whole kingdom. The word imports what the Latins call *nanunculus*, the Italians *homunceletino*, and the English *mannikin*. To her I chiefly owe my preservation in that country. We never parted while I was there; I called her my Glumdalclitch, or little nurse; and should be guilty of great ingratitude if I omitted this honorable mention of her care and affection towards me, which I heartily wish it lay in my power to requite as she deserves.

It now began to be known and talked of in the neighborhood, that my master had found a strange animal in the field, about the bigness of a *splacnuck*, but exactly shaped in every part like a human creature; which it likewise imitated in all its actions, seemed to speak in a little language of its own, had already learned several words of theirs, went erect upon two legs, was tame and gentle, would come when it was called, do whatever it was bid, had the finest limbs in the world, and a complexion fairer than a nobleman's daughter of three years old. Another farmer, who lived hard by, and was a particular friend of my master, came on a visit on purpose to inquire into the truth of this story. I was immediately produced and placed upon a table, where I walked as I was commanded, drew my hanger, put it up again, made my reverence to my master's guest, asked him in his own language how he did, and told him *he was welcome*, just as my little nurse had instructed me. This man, who was old and dim-sighted, put on his spectacles to behold me better, at which I could not forbear laughing very heartily, for his eyes appeared like the full moon shining into a chamber at two windows. Our people, who discovered the cause of my mirth, bore me company in laughing, at which the old fellow was fool enough to be angry and out of countenance. He had the character of a great miser; and, to my misfortune, he well deserved it by the cursed advice he gave my master, to show me as a sight upon a market-day in the next town, which was half an hour's riding, about two-and-twenty miles from our house. I guessed there was some mischief contriving, when I observed my master and his friend whispering long together, sometimes pointing at me; and my fears made me

fancy that I overheard and understood some of their words.

"I CALLED HER MY GLUMDALCLITCH."

But the next morning, Glumdalclitch, my little nurse, told me the whole matter, which she had cunningly picked out from her mother. The poor girl laid me on her bosom, and fell a-weeping with shame and grief. She apprehended some mischief would happen to me from rude vulgar folks, who might squeeze me to death, or break one of my limbs by taking me in their hands. She had also observed how modest I was in my nature, how nicely I regarded my honor, and what an indignity conceive it to be exposed for money, as a public spectacle, to the meanest of the people. She said her papa and mamma had promised that Grildrig should be hers, but now she found they meant to serve her as they did last year when they pretended to give her a lamb, and yet as soon as it was fat sold it to a butcher. For my own part I may truly affirm that I was less concerned than my nurse. I had a strong hope, which left me, that I should one day recover my liberty; to the ignominy of being carried about for a monster, I considered myself to be a perfect stranger in the country, and that such a misfortune could never be charged upon me as a reproach if ever I should return to England; since the king of Great Britain himself, in my condition, must have undergone the same distress.

My master, pursuant to the advice of his friend, carried me in a box the next market-day, to the neighboring town, and took along with him his little daughter, my nurse, upon a pillion[48] behind him. The box was close on every side, with a little door for me to go in and out, and a few gimlet holes to let in air. The girl had been so careful as to put the quilt of her baby's bed into it, for me to lie down on. However, I was terribly shaken and discomposed in this journey, though it were but of half an hour. For the horse went about forty feet at every step, and trotted so high that the agitation was equal to the rising and falling of a ship in a great storm, but much more frequent; our journey was somewhat farther than from London to St. Alban's. My master alighted at an inn which he used to frequent; and after consulting a while with the innkeeper and making some necessary preparations, he hired the *grultrud*, or crier, to give notice through the town, of a strange creature to be seen at the sign of the Green Eagle, not so big as a *splacnuck* (an animal in that country, very finely shaped, about six feet long), and in every part of the body resembling a human creature, could speak several words, and perform a hundred diverting tricks.

I was placed upon a table in the largest room of the inn, which might be near three hundred feet square. My little nurse stood on a low stool close to the table, to take care of me, and direct what I should do. My master, to avoid a crowd, would suffer only thirty people at a time to see me. I walked about on the table as the girl commanded. She asked me questions, as far as she knew my understanding of the language reached, and I answered them as loud as I could. I turned about several times to the company, paid my humble respects, said they were welcome, and used some other speeches I had been taught. I took a thimble filled with liquor, which Glumdalclitch had given me for a cup, and drank their health. I drew out my hanger, and flourished with it, after the manner of fencers in England. My nurse gave me part of a straw, which I exercised as a pike, having learnt the art in my youth. I was that day shown to twelve sets of company, and as often forced to act over again the same fopperies, till I was half dead with weariness and vexation. For those who had seen me made such wonderful reports, that the people were ready to break down the doors to come in.

My master, for his own interest, would not suffer any one to touch me except my nurse, and, to prevent danger, benches were set round the table at such a distance as to put me out of everybody's reach. However, an unlucky school-boy aimed a hazel-nut directly at my head, which very narrowly missed me: otherwise, it came with so much violence, that it would have infallibly knocked out my brains, for it was almost as large as a small pumpion,[49] but I had the satisfaction to see the young rogue well beaten, and turned out of the room.

"FLOURISHED IT AFTER THE MANNER OF FENCERS IN ENGLAND."

My master gave public notice that he would show me again the next market-day, and in the meantime he prepared a more convenient vehicle for me, which he had reason enough to do; for I was so tired with my first journey, and with entertaining company for eight hours together, that I could hardly stand upon my legs or speak a word. It was at least three days before I recovered my strength; and that I might have no rest at home, all the neighboring gentleman, from a hundred miles round, hearing of my fame, came to see me at my master's own house. There could not be fewer than thirty persons with their wives and children (for the country was very populous); and my master demanded the rate of a full room whenever he showed me at home, although it were only to a single family; so that for some time I had but little ease every day of the week (except Wednesday which is their Sabbath), although I was not carried to the town.

My master, finding how profitable I was like to be, resolved to carry me to the most considerable cities of the kingdom. Having, therefore, provided himself with all things necessary for a long journey, and settled his affairs at home, he took leave of his wife, and upon the seventeenth of August, 1703, about two months after my arrival, we set out for the metropolis, situated the middle of that empire, and about three thousand miles distance from our house. My master made his daughter Glumdalclitch ride behind him. She carried me on her lap, in a box tied about her waist. The girl had lined it on all sides with the softest cloth she could get, well quilted underneath, furnished it

78

with her baby's bed, provided me with linen and other necessaries, and made everything as conveniently as she could. We had no other company but a boy of the house, who rode after us with the luggage.

My master's design was to show me in all the towns by the way, and to step out of the road for fifty or a hundred miles, to any village, or person of quality's house, where he might expect custom. We made easy journeys of not above seven or eight score miles a day; for Glumdalclitch, on purpose to spare me, complained she was tired with the trotting of the horse. She often took me out of my box at my own desire, to give me air and show me the country, but always held me fast by a leading-string. We passed over five or six rivers, many degrees broader and deeper than the Nile or the Ganges; and there was hardly a rivulet so small as the Thames at London Bridge. We were ten weeks in our journey, and I was shown in eighteen large towns, besides many villages and private families.

On the twenty-sixth of October we arrived at the metropolis, called in their language, *Lorbrulgrud*, or Pride of the Universe. My master took a lodging in the principal street of the city, not far from the royal palace, and put out bills in the usual form, containing an exact description of my person and parts.[50] He hired a large room between three and four hundred feet wide. He provided a table sixty feet in diameter, upon which I was to act my part, and palisadoed it round three feet from the edge, and as many high, to prevent my falling over. I was shown ten times a day, to the wonder and satisfaction of all people. I could now speak the language tolerably well, and perfectly understood every word that was spoken to me. Besides, I had learned their alphabet, and could make a shift to explain a sentence here and there; for Glumdalclitch had been my instructor while we were at home, and at leisure hours during our journey. She carried a little book in her pocket, not much larger than a Sanson's Atlas;[51] it was a common treatise for the use of young girls, giving a short account of their religion; out of this she taught me my letters, and interpreted the words.

[48] *Pillion*: a cushion for a woman to ride on behind a person on horseback. *From London to St. Alban's*: about twenty miles.

[49] *Pumpion*: pumpkin.

[50] *Parts*: accomplishments.

[51] *Sanson's Atlas*: a very large atlas by a French geographer in use in Swift's time.

CHAPTER III.

The Author Sent for to Court. the Queen Buys Him of His Master the Farmer, and Presents Him to the King. He Disputes With His Majesty's Great Scholars. an Apartment at Court Provided for the Author. He is in High Favor With the Queen. He Stands Up for the Honor of His Own Country. He Quarrels With the Queen's Dwarf.

The frequent labors I underwent every day, made in a few weeks a very considerable change in my health; the more my master got by me, the more insatiable he grew. I had quite lost my stomach, and was almost reduced to a skeleton. The farmer observed it, and, concluding I must soon die, resolved to make as good a hand of me[52] as he could. While he was thus reasoning and resolving with himself, a *slardral*, or gentleman-usher, came from court, commanding my master to carry me immediately thither, for the diversion of the queen and her ladies. Some of the latter had already been to see me, and reported strange things of my beauty, behavior, and good sense. Her majesty, and those who attended her, were beyond measure delighted with my demeanor. I fell on my knees and begged the honor of kissing her imperial foot; but this gracious princess held out her little finger towards me, after I was set on a table, which I embraced in both my arms, and put the tip of it with the utmost respect to my lip.

She made me some general questions about my country, and my travels, which I answered as distinctly, and in as few words, as I could. She asked whether I would be content to live at court. I bowed down to the board of the table, and humbly answered that I was my master's slave; but if I were at my own disposal, I should be proud to devote my life to her majesty's service. She then asked my master whether he were willing to sell me at a good price. He, who apprehended I could not live a month, was ready enough to part with me, and demanded a thousand pieces of gold, which were ordered him on the spot, each piece being the bigness of eight hundred moidores[53]; but, for the proportion of all things between that country and Europe, and the high price of gold among them, was hardly so great a sum as a thousand guineas[54] would be in England. I then said to the queen, since I was now her majesty's most humble creature and vassal, I must beg the favor, that Glumdalclitch, who had always attended me with so much care and kindness, and understood to do it so well, might be admitted into her service, and continue to be my nurse and instructor.

Her majesty agreed to my petition, and easily got the farmer's consent, who was glad enough to have his daughter preferred at court, and the poor girl herself was not able to hide her joy. My late master withdrew, bidding me farewell, and saying he had left me in good service, to which I replied not a word, only making him a slight bow.

"THIS GRACIOUS PRINCESS HELD OUT HER LITTLE FINGER."

The queen observed my coldness, and, when the farmer was gone out of the apartment, asked me the reason. I made bold to tell her majesty that I owed no other obligation to my late master, than his not dashing out the brains of a poor harmless creature, found by chance in his field; which obligation was amply recompensed by the gain he had made in showing me through half the kingdom, and the price he had now sold me for. That the life I had since led was laborious enough to kill an animal of ten times my strength. That my health was much impaired by the continual drudgery of entertaining the rabble every hour of the day, and that, if my master had not thought my life in danger, her majesty would not have got so cheap a bargain. But as I was out of all fear of being ill-treated under the protection of so great and good an empress, the ornament of nature, the darling of the world, the delight of her subjects, the phoenix[55] of the creation; so, I hoped my late master's apprehensions would appear to be groundless, for I already found my spirits to revive, by the influence of her most august presence.

This was the sum of my speech, delivered with great improprieties and hesitation; the latter part was altogether framed in the style peculiar to that people, whereof I learned some phrases from Glumdalclitch, while she was carrying me to court.

The queen, giving great allowance for my defectiveness in speaking, was, however, surprised at so much wit and good sense in so diminutive an animal.

82

"SHE ... CARRIED ME TO THE KING."

She took me in her own hand, and carried me to the king, who was then retired to his cabinet.[56] His majesty, a prince of much gravity and austere countenance, not well observing my shape at first view, asked the queen, after a cold manner, how long it was since she grew fond of a *splacnuck*; for such it seems he took me to be, as I lay upon my breast in her majesty's right hand. But this princess, who hath an infinite deal of wit and humor, set me gently on my feet upon the scrutoire,[57] and commanded me to give his majesty an account of myself, which I did in a very few words; and Glumdalclitch, who attended at the cabinet–door, and could not endure I should be out of her sight, being admitted, confirmed all that had passed from my arrival at her father's house.

The king, although he be as learned a person as any in his dominions, had been educated in the study of philosophy, and particularly mathematics; yet, when he observed my shape exactly, and saw me walk erect, before I began to speak, conceived I might be a piece of clockwork (which is in that country arrived to a very great perfection) contrived by some ingenious artist. But when he heard my voice, and found what I delivered to be regular and rational, he could not conceal his astonishment. He was by no means satisfied with the relation I gave him of the manner I came into his kingdom, but thought it a story concerted between Glumdalclitch and her father, who had taught me a set of words, to make me sell at a better price. Upon this imagination he put several other questions to me, and still received rational answers, no otherwise defective than by a foreign accent, and an imperfect knowledge in the language, with some rustic phrases, which I had learned at the farmer's house, and did not suit the polite style of a court.

His majesty sent for three great scholars, who were then in their weekly waiting[58] according to the custom in that country. These gentlemen, after they had a while examined my shape with much nicety, were of different opinions concerning me. They all agreed that I could not be produced according to the regular laws of nature, because I was not framed with a capacity of preserving my life, either by swiftness or climbing of trees, or digging holes in the earth. They observed by my teeth, which they viewed with great exactness, that I was a carnivorous animal; yet most quadrupeds being an overmatch for me, and field-mice, with some others, too nimble, they could not imagine how I should be able to support myself, unless I fed upon snails and other insects, which they offered, by many learned arguments, to evince that I could not possibly do. They would not allow me to be a dwarf, because my littleness was beyond all degrees of comparison; for the queen's favorite dwarf, the smallest ever known in that kingdom, was nearly thirty feet high. After much debate, they concluded unanimously that I was only *relplum scalcath*, which is interpreted literally, *lusus naturae*;[59] a determination exactly agreeable to the modern philosophy of Europe: whose professors, disdaining the old evasion of occult causes, whereby the followers of Aristotle endeavored in vain to disguise their ignorance, have invented this wonderful solution of all difficulties, to the unspeakable advancement of human knowledge.

After this decisive conclusion, I entreated to be heard a word or two. I applied myself to the king, and assured his majesty that I came from a country which abounded with several millions of both sexes, and of my own stature; where the animals, trees, and houses were all in proportion, and where, by consequence, I might be as able to defend myself, and to find sustenance, as any of his majesty's subjects could do here; which I took for a full answer to those gentlemen's arguments. To this they only replied with a smile of contempt, saying, that the farmer had instructed me very well in my lesson. The king, who had a much better understanding, dismissing his learned men, sent for the farmer, who, by good fortune, was not yet gone out of town; having therefore first examined him privately, and then confronted him with me and the young girl, his majesty began to think that what we had told him might possibly be true. He desired the queen to order that a particular care should be taken of me, and was of opinion that Glumdalclitch should still continue in her office of tending me, because he observed that we had a great affection for each other. A convenient apartment was provided for her at court; she had a sort of governess appointed to take care of her education, a maid to dress her, and two other servants for menial offices; but the care of me was wholly appropriated to herself. The queen commanded her own cabinet-maker to contrive a box, that might serve me for a bed-chamber, after the model that Glumdalclitch and I should agree upon. This man was a most ingenious artist, and, according to my directions, in three weeks finished to me a wooden chamber of sixteen feet square and twelve high, with sash-windows, a door, and two closets, like a London bed-chamber. The board that made the ceiling was to be lifted up and down by two hinges, to put in a bed ready furnished by her majesty's upholsterer, which Glumdalclitch took out every day to air, made it with her own hands, and, letting it down at night, locked up the roof over me. A nice workman, who was famous for little curiosities, undertook to make me two chairs, with backs and frames, of a substance not unlike ivory, and two tables, with a cabinet to put my things in. The room was quilted on all sides, as well as the floor and the ceiling, to prevent any accident from the carelessness of those who carried me, and to break the force of a jolt when I went in a coach. I desired a lock for my door, to prevent rats and mice from coming in: the smith, after several attempts, made the smallest that ever was seen among them; for I have known a larger at the gate of a gentleman's house in England. I made a shift to keep the key in a pocket of my own, fearing Glumdalclitch might lose it. The queen likewise ordered the thinnest silks that could be gotten to make me clothes, not much thicker than an English blanket, very cumbersome, till I was accustomed to them. They were after the fashion of the kingdom, partly resembling the Persian, and partly the Chinese, and are a very grave and decent habit.

The queen became so fond of my company that she could not dine without me. I had a table placed upon the same at which her Majesty ate, just at her left elbow, and a chair to sit on. Glumdalclitch stood on a stool on the floor, near my table, to assist and take care of me. I had an entire set of silver dishes and plates, and other necessaries, which, in proportion to those of the queen, were not much bigger than what I have seen in a London toy-shop for the furniture of a baby-house: these my little nurse kept in her pocket in a silver box, and gave me at meals as I wanted them, always cleaning them herself. No person dined with the queen but the two princesses royal the elder sixteen years old, and the younger at that time thirteen and a month. Her majesty used to put a bit of meat upon one of my dishes, out of which I carved for myself: and her diversion was to see me eat in miniature; for the queen (who had, indeed, but a weak stomach) took up at one mouthful as much as a dozen English farmers could eat at a meal, which to me was for some time a very nauseous sight. She would craunch the wing of a lark, bones and all, between her teeth, although it were nine times as large as that of a full-grown turkey; and put a bit of bread in her mouth as big as two twelve-penny loaves. She drank out of a golden cup, above a hogshead at a draught. Her knives were twice as long as a scythe, set straight upon the handle. The spoons, forks, and other instruments, were all in the same proportion. I remember when Glumdalclitch carried me, out of curiosity, to see some of the tables at court, where ten or a dozen of these enormous knives and forks were lifted up together, I thought I had never till then beheld so terrible a sight.

It is the custom that every Wednesday (which, as I have before observed, is their Sabbath) the king and queen, with the royal issue of both sexes dine together in the apartment of his majesty, to whom I was now become a great favorite; and, at these times, my little chair and table were placed at his left hand, before one of the salt-cellars. This prince took a pleasure in conversing with me, inquiring into the manners, religion, taws, government, and learning of Europe; wherein I gave him the best account I was able. His apprehension was so clear, and his judgment so exact, that he made very wise reflections and observations upon all I said. But I confess that after I had been a little too copious in talking of my own beloved country, of our trade, and wars by sea and land, of our schisms in religion, and parties in the state; the prejudices of his education prevailed so far that he could not forbear taking me up in his right hand, and, stroking me gently with the other, after a hearty fit of laughing, asked me, whether I was a whig or a tory? Then turning to his first minister, who waited behind him with a white staff, near as tall as the mainmast of the "Royal Sovereign[60]," he observed how contemptible a thing was human grandeur, which could be mimicked by such diminutive insects as I: and yet, says he, I dare engage these creatures have their titles and distinctions of honor; they contrive little nests and burrows, that they call houses and cities; they make a figure in dress and equipage; they love, they fight, they dispute, they cheat, they betray. And thus he continued on, while my color came and went several times with indignation, to hear our noble country, the mistress of arts and arms, the scourge of France, the arbitress of Europe, the seat of virtue, piety, honor, and truth, the pride and envy of the world, so contemptuously treated.

But, as I was not in a condition to resent injuries, so upon mature thoughts, I began to doubt whether I was injured or no. For, after having been accustomed, several months, to the sight and converse of this people, and observed every object upon which I cast mine eyes to be of proportionable magnitude, the horror I had at first conceived from their bulk and aspect was so far worn off, that, if I had then beheld a company of English lords and ladies in their finery, and birthday clothes, acting their several parts in the most courtly manner of strutting and bowing and prating, to say the truth, I should have been strongly tempted to laugh as much at them as the king and his grandees did at me. Neither, indeed, could I forbear smiling at myself, when the queen used to place me upon her hand towards a looking-glass, by which both our persons appeared before me in full view together; and there could nothing be more ridiculous than the comparison; so that I really began to imagine myself dwindled many degrees below my usual size.

Nothing angered and mortified me so much, as the queen's dwarf, who being of the lowest stature that ever in that country (for I verily think he was not full thirty feet high) became so insolent at seeing a creature so much beneath him, that he would always affect to swagger, and look big, as he passed by me in the queen's ante-chamber, while I was standing on some table, talking with the lords or ladies of the court, and he seldom failed of a smart word or two upon my littleness; against which I could only revenge myself, by calling him brother, challenging him to wrestle, and such repartees as are usual in the mouths of court pages. One day, at dinner, this malicious little cub was so nettled with something I had said to him, that, raising himself upon the frame of her majesty's chair, he took me up, as I was sitting down, not thinking any harm; and let me drop into a large silver bowl of cream, and then ran away as fast as he could. I fell over head and ears, and, if I had not been a good swimmer, it might have gone very hard with me; for Glumdalclitch, in that instant, happened to be at the other end of the room, and the queen was in such a fright, that she wanted presence of mind to assist me. But my little nurse ran to my relief, and took me out, after I had swallowed above a quart of cream. I was put to bed; however, I received no other damage than the loss of a suit of clothes, which was utterly spoiled. The dwarf was soundly whipped, and, as a farther punishment, forced to drink up the bowl of cream into which he had thrown me; neither was he ever restored to favor; for, soon after, the queen bestowed him on a lady of high quality, so that I saw him no more, to my very great satisfaction; for I could not tell to what extremity such a malicious urchin might have carried his resentment.

"I COULD ONLY REVENGE MYSELF BY CALLING HIM BROTHER."

He had before served me a scurvy trick, which set the queen a-laughing, although, at the same time she was heartily vexed, and would have immediately cashiered him, if I had not been so generous as to intercede. Her majesty had taken a marrow-bone upon her plate and, after knocking out the marrow, placed the bone on the dish erect, as it stood before. The dwarf watching his opportunity, while Glumdalclitch was gone to the sideboard, mounted upon the stool she stood on to take care of me at meals, took me up in both hands, and, squeezing my legs together, wedged them into the marrow-bone above my waist, where I stuck for some time, and made a very ridiculous figure, I believe it was near a minute before any one knew what was became of me; for I thought it below me to cry out. But, as princes seldom get their meat hot, my legs were not scalded, only my stockings and breeches in a sad condition. The dwarf, at my entreaty, had no other punishment than a sound whipping.

I was frequently rallied by the queen upon account of my fearfulness; and she used to ask me, whether the people of my country were as great cowards as myself? The occasion was this; the kingdom is much pestered with flies in summer; and these odious insects, each of them as big as a Dunstable lark,[61] hardly gave me any rest, while I sat at dinner, with their continual humming and buzzing about my ears. They would sometimes alight upon my victuals. Sometimes they would fix upon my nose or forehead, where they stung me to the quick, and I had much ado to defend myself against these detestable animals, and could not forbear starting when they came on my face. It was the common practice of the dwarf, to catch a number of these insects in his hand, as school-boys do among us, and let them out suddenly under my nose, on purpose to frighten me, and divert the queen. My remedy was, to cut them in pieces with my knife, as they flew in the air, wherein my dexterity was much admired.

I remember, one morning, when Glumdalclitch had set me in my box upon a window, as she usually did in fair days, to give me air (for I durst not venture to let the box be hung on a nail out of the window, as we do with cages in England) after I had lifted up one of my sashes, and sat down at my table to eat a piece of sweet-cake for my breakfast, above twenty wasps, allured by the smell, came flying into the room, humming louder than the drones[62] of as many bag-pipes. Some of them seized my cake, and carried it piece-meal away; others flew about my head and face, confounding me with the noise, and putting me in the utmost terror of their stings. However, I had the courage to rise and draw my hanger, and attack them in the air. I despatched four of them, but the rest got away, and I presently shut my window. These creatures were as large as partridges; I took out their stings, found them an inch and a half long, and as sharp as needles. I carefully preserved them all, and having since shown them, with some other curiosities, in several parts of Europe, upon my return to England, I gave

three of them to Gresham College,[53] and kept the fourth for myself.

---

[52] *As good a hand of me*: as much money of me.

[53] *Moidore*: a Portuguese gold piece worth about six dollars.

[54] *Guineas*: an obsolete English gold coin, of the value of five dollars.

[55] *Phoenix*: a bird of fable said to live for a long time and rise anew from its own ashes.

[56] *Cabinet*: a private room.

[57] *Scrutoire*: a writing-desk.

[58] *Waiting*: attendance on the king.

[59] *Lusus naturae*: a freak of nature.

[60] *Royal Sovereign*: one of the great ships of Swift's time.

[61] *Dunstable lark:* large larks are caught on the downs near Dunstable between September and February, and sent to London for luxurious tables.

[62] *Drone:* the largest tube of a bag-pipe, giving forth a dull heavy tone.

[63] *Gresham College*, in London, is named after the founder, an English merchant, who died in 1579.

CHAPTER IV.

The Country Described. a Proposal for Correcting Modern Maps.
the King's Palace, and Some Account of the Metropolis. the
Author's Way of Travelling. the Chief Temple Described.

I now intend to give the reader a short description of this country, as far as I travelled in it, which was not above two thousand miles round Lorbrulgrud, the metropolis. For the queen, whom I always attended, never went farther when she accompanied the king in his progresses, and there staid till his majesty returned from viewing his frontiers. The whole extent of this prince's dominions reacheth about six thousand miles in length, and from three to five in breadth. From whence I cannot but conclude, that our geographers of Europe are in a great error, by supposing nothing but sea between Japan and California; for it was ever my opinion, that there must be a balance of earth to counterpoise the great continent of Tartary; and therefore they ought to correct their maps and charts, by joining this vast tract of land to the northwest parts of America, wherein I shall be ready to lend them my assistance.

The kingdom is a peninsula, terminated to the northeast by a ridge of mountains, thirty miles high, which are altogether impassable, by reason of the volcanoes upon the tops: neither do the most learned know what sort of mortals inhabit beyond those mountains, or whether they be inhabited at all. On the three other sides it is bounded by the ocean. There is not one sea-port in the whole kingdom, and those parts of the coasts into which the rivers issue, are so full of pointed rocks, and the sea generally so rough, that there is no venturing with the smallest of their boats; so that these people are wholly excluded from any commerce with the rest of the world.

But the large rivers are full of vessels, and abound with excellent fish, for they seldom get any from the sea, because the sea-fish are of the same size with those in Europe, and consequently not worth catching, whereby it is manifest, that nature, in the production of plants and animals of so extraordinary a bulk, is wholly confined to this continent, of which I leave the reasons to be determined by philosophers. However, now and then, they take a whale, that happens to be dashed against the rocks, which the common people feed on heartily. These whales I have known so large, that a man could hardly carry one upon his shoulders; and sometimes, for curiosity, they are brought in hampers to Lorbrulgrud: I saw one of them in a dish at the king's table, which passed for a rarity, but I did not observe he was fond of it; for I think indeed the bigness disgusted him, although I have seen one somewhat larger in Greenland.

The country is well inhabited, for it contains fifty-one cities, near a hundred walled towns, and a great number of villages. To satisfy my curious reader, it may be sufficient to describe Lorbrulgrud. This city stands upon almost two equal parts on each side the river that passes through. It contains above eighty thousand houses, and about six hundred thousand inhabitants. It is in length three *glomglungs* (which make about fifty-four English miles) and two and a half in breadth, as I measured it myself in the royal map made by the king's order, which was laid on the ground on purpose for me, and extended a hundred feet: I paced the diameter and circumference several times barefoot, and, computing by the scale, measured it pretty exactly.

The king's palace is no regular edifice, but a heap of buildings, about seven miles round: the chief rooms are generally two hundred and forty feet high, and broad and long in proportion. A coach was allowed to Glumdalclitch and me, wherein her governess frequently took her out to see the town, or go among the shops; and I was always of the party, carried in my box; although the girl, at my own desire, would often take me out, and hold me in her hand, that I might more conveniently view the houses and the people as we passed along the streets, I reckoned our coach to be about the square of Westminster-hall, but not altogether so high: however, I cannot be very exact.

Besides the large box in which I was usually carried, the queen ordered a smaller one to be made for me, of about twelve feet square and ten high, for the convenience of travelling, because the other was somewhat too large for Glumdalclitch's lap, and cumbersome in the coach. It was made by the same artist, whom I directed in the whole contrivance. This travelling closet was an exact square,[64] with a window in the middle of three of the squares, and each window was latticed with iron wire on the outside, to prevent accidents in long journeys. On the fourth side, which had no window, two strong staples were fixed, through which the person who carried me, when I had a mind to be on horseback, put a leathern belt, and buckled it about his waist. This was always the office of some grave, trusty servant, in whom I could confide, whether I attended the king and queen in their progresses, or were disposed to see the gardens, or pay a visit to some great lady or minister of state in the court; for I soon began to be known and esteemed among the greatest officers, I suppose more on account of their majesties' favor than any merit of my own.

In journeys, when I was weary of the coach, a servant on horseback would buckle on my box, and place it upon a cushion before him; and there I had a full prospect of the country on three sides from my three windows. I had in this closet a field-bed, and a hammock hung from the ceiling, two chairs and a table, neatly screwed to the floor, to prevent being tossed about by the agitation of the horse or the coach. And having been long used to sea voyages, those motions, although sometimes very violent, did not much discompose me.

Whenever I had a mind to see the town, it was always in my travelling closet, which Glumdalclitch held in her lap, in a kind of open sedan, after the fashion of the country, borne by four men, and attended by two others in the queen's livery. The people, who had often heard of me, were very curious to crowd about the sedan, and the girl was complaisant enough to make the bearers stop, and to take me in her hand, that I might be more conveniently seen.

I was very desirous to see the chief temple, and particularly the tower belonging to it, which is reckoned the highest in the kingdom. Accordingly, one day my nurse carried me thither, but I must truly say I came back disappointed; for the height is not above three thousand feet, reckoning from the ground to the highest pinnacle top; which, allowing for the difference between the size of those people and us in Europe, is no great matter for admiration, nor at all equal in proportion (if I rightly remember) to Salisbury steeple.[65] But, not to detract from a nation, to which during my life I shall acknowledge myself extremely obliged, it must be allowed that whatever this famous tower wants in height is amply made up in beauty and strength. For the walls are nearly a hundred feet thick, built of hewn stone, whereof each is about forty feet square, and adorned on all sides with statues of gods and emperors, cut in marble larger than life, placed in their several niches. I measured a little finger which had fallen down from one of these statues, and lay unperceived among some rubbish, and found it exactly four feet and an inch in length. Glumdalclitch wrapped it up in her handkerchief and carried it home in her pocket, to keep among other trinkets, of which the girl was very fond, as children at her age usually are.

The king's kitchen is indeed a noble building, vaulted at top, and about six hundred feet high. The great oven is not so wide by ten paces as the cupola at St. Paul's, for I measured the latter on purpose after my return. But if I should describe the kitchen-grate, the prodigious pots and kettles, the joints of meat turning on the spits, with many other particulars, perhaps I should be hardly believed; at least, a severe critic would be apt to think I enlarged a little, as travellers are often suspected to do. To avoid which censure, I fear I have run too much into the other extreme; and that if this treatise should happen to be translated into the language of Brobdingnag (which is the general name of that kingdom) and transmitted thither, the king and his people would have reason to complain that I had done them an injury, by a false and diminutive representation.

His majesty seldom keeps above six hundred horses in his stables: they are generally from fifty-four to sixty feet high. But when he goes abroad on solemn days, he is attended for state by a militia guard of five hundred horse, which indeed I thought was the most splendid sight that could be ever beheld, till I saw part of his army in battalia,[66] whereof I shall find another occasion to speak.

---

[64] *The square of*: as large as the square of.

[65] *Salisbury Steeple*: this is about four hundred feet high.

[66] *Battalia*: the order of battle.

CHAPTER V.

Several Adventures That Happened to the Author. the Author Shows His Skill in Navigation.

I should have lived happily enough in that country, if my littleness had not exposed me to several ridiculous and troublesome accidents, some of which I shall venture to relate. Glumdalclitch often carried me into the gardens of the court in my smaller box, and would sometimes take me out of it, and hold me in her hand, or set me down to walk. I remember, before the dwarf left the queen, he followed us one day into those gardens, and my nurse having set me down, he and I being close together, near some dwarf apple-trees, I must needs show my wit by a silly allusion between him and the trees, which happens to hold in their language, as it doth in ours. Whereupon the malicious rogue, watching his opportunity, when I was walking under one of them, shook it directly over my head; by which a dozen apples, each of them near as large as a Bristol barrel, came tumbling about my ears; one of them hit me on the back as I chanced to stoop, and knocked me down flat on my face; but I received no other hurt; and the dwarf was pardoned at my desire, because I had given the provocation.

Another day, Glumdalclitch left me on a smooth grass-plot to divert myself, while she walked at some distance with her governess. In the meantime there suddenly fell such a violent shower of hail, that I was immediately, by the force of it, struck to the ground; and when I was down, the hail stones gave me such cruel bangs all over the body as if I had been pelted with tennis-balls, however, I made a shift to creep on all fours, and

95

shelter myself by lying flat on my face on the lee-side of a border of lemon-thyme, but so bruised from head to foot that I could not go abroad in ten days. Neither is this at all to be wondered at, because nature, in that country, observing the same proportion through all her operations, a hail-stone is near eighteen hundred times as large as one in Europe, which I can assert upon experience, having been so curious to weigh and measure them.

But a more dangerous accident happened to me in the same garden, when my little nurse, believing she had put me in a secure place, which I often entreated her to do, that I might enjoy my own thoughts, and having left my box at home, to avoid the trouble of carrying it, went to another part of the garden with governess and some ladies of her acquaintance, she was absent and out of hearing, a small white belonging to one of the chief gardeners, having got by accident into the garden, happened to place where I lay: the dog, following the scent, came directly up, and taking me in his mouth, ran straight to his master, wagging his tail, and set me gently on the ground. By good fortune, he had been so well taught, that I was carried between his teeth without the least hurt, or even tearing my clothes. But the poor gardener, who knew me well, and had a great kindness for me, was in a terrible fright: he gently took me up in both his hands, and asked me how I did; but I was so amazed and out of breath, that I could not speak a word. In a few minutes I came to myself, and he carried me safe to my little nurse, who by this time had returned to the place where she left me, and was in cruel agonies when I did not appear nor answer when she called. She severely reprimanded the gardener on account of his dog, but the thing was bushed up and never known at court; for the girl was afraid of the queen's anger, and truly, as to myself, I thought it would not be for my reputation that such a story should go about.

This accident absolutely determined Glumdalclitch never to trust me abroad for the future out of her sight. I had been long afraid of this resolution, and therefore concealed from her some little unlucky adventures that happened in those times when I was left by myself. Once a kite, hovering over the garden, made a stoop at me; and if I had not resolutely drawn my hanger, and run under a thick espalier,[67] he would have certainly carried me away in his talons. Another time, walking to the top of a fresh mole-hill, I fell to my neck in the hole through which that animal had cast up the earth. I likewise broke my right shin against the shell of a snail, which I happened to stumble over as I was walking alone and thinking on poor England.

I cannot tell whether I were more pleased or mortified to observe in those solitary walks that the smaller birds did not appear to be at all afraid of me, but would hop about within a yard's distance, looking for worms and other food, with as much indifference and security as if no creature at all were near them. I remember a thrush had the confidence to snatch out of my hand with his bill a piece of cake that Glumdalclitch had just given me for my breakfast.

When I attempted to catch any of these birds they would boldly turn against me, endeavoring to pick my fingers, which I durst not venture within their reach; and then they would hop back unconcerned to hunt for worms and snails as they did before. But one day I took a thick cudgel, and threw it with all my strength so luckily at a linnet that I knocked him down, and seizing him by the neck with both my hands ran with him in triumph to my nurse. However, the bird, who had only been stunned, recovering himself, gave me so many boxes with his wings on both sides of my head and body, though I held him at arm's length and was out of the reach of his claws, that I was twenty times thinking of letting him go. But I was soon relieved by one of our servants, who wrung off the bird's neck, and I had him next day for dinner by the queen's command. This linnet, as near as I can remember, seemed to be somewhat larger than an English swan.

The queen, who often used to hear me talk of my sea-voyages, and took all occasions to divert me when I was melancholy, asked me, whether I understood how to handle a sail or an oar, and whether a little exercise of rowing might not be convenient for my health. I answered, that I understood both very well; for, although nay proper employment had been to be surgeon or doctor to the ship, yet often, upon a pinch, I was forced to work like a common mariner. But I could not see how this could be done in their country, where the smallest wherry was equal to a first-rate man-of-war among us, and such a boat as I could manage would never live in any of their rivers.

"THE SMALLER BIRDS DID NOT APPEAR TO BE AT ALL AFRAID OF ME."

Her majesty said, if I could contrive a boat, her own joiner should make it, and she would provide a place for me to sail in. The fellow was an ingenious workman, and, by my instructions, in ten days finished a pleasure-boat, with all its tackling, able conveniently to hold eight Europeans. When it was finished, the queen was so delighted that she ran with it in her lap to the king, who ordered it to be put in a cistern full of water, with me in it, by way of trial; where I could not manage my two sculls,[68] or little oars, for want of room.

But the queen had before contrived another project. She ordered the joiner to make a wooden trough of three hundred feet long, fifty broad, and eight deep; which, being well pitched, to prevent leaking, was placed on the floor along the wall in an outer room of the palace. It had a cock near the bottom to let out the water, when it began to grow stale; and two servants could easily fill it in half-an-hour. Here I often used to row for my own diversion, as well as that of the queen and her ladies, who thought themselves well entertained with my skill and agility. Sometimes I would put up my sail, and then my business was only to steer, while the ladies gave me a gale with their fans; and when they were weary, some of their pages would blow my sail forward with their breath, while I showed my art by steering starboard[69] or larboard, as I pleased. When I had done, Glumdalclitch always carried back my boat, into her closet, and hung it oh a nail to dry.

In this exercise I once met an accident, which had like to have cost me my life; for one of the pages having put my boat into the trough, the governess, who attended Glumdalclitch, very officiously lifted me up to place me in the boat, but I happened to slip through her fingers, and should infallibly have fallen down forty feet upon the floor, if, by the luckiest chance in the world, I had not been stopped by a corking-pin[70] that stuck in the good gentlewoman's stomacher;[71] the head of the pin passed between my shirt and the waistband of my breeches, and thus I held by the middle in the air, till Glumdalclitch ran to my relief.

"GAVE ME A GALE WITH THEIR FANS."

Another time, one of the servants, whose office it was to fill my trough every third day with fresh water, was so careless as to let a huge frog (not perceiving it) slip out of his pail. The frog lay concealed till I was put into my boat, but then seeing a resting-place, climbed up, and made it lean so much on one side that I was forced to balance it with all my weight on the other to prevent overturning. When the frog was got in, it hopped at once half the length of the boat, and then over my head backwards and forwards. The largeness of its features made it appear the most deformed animal that can be conceived. However, I desired Glumdalclitch to let me deal with it alone. I banged it a good while with one of my sculls, and at last forced it to leap out of the boat.

But the greatest danger I ever underwent in that kingdom was from a monkey, who belonged to one of the clerks of the kitchen. Glumdalclitch had locked the up in her closet, while she went somewhere upon business or a visit. The weather being very warm the closet window was left open, as well as the windows and the door of my bigger box, in which I usually lived, because of its largeness and conveniency. As I sat quietly meditating at my table, I heard something bounce in at the closet window, and skip about from one side to the other; whereat, although I was much alarmed, yet I ventured to look out, but not stirring from my seat; and then I saw this frolicsome animal frisking and leaping up and down, till at last he came to my box, which he seemed to view with great pleasure and curiosity, peeping in at the door and every window.

I retreated to the farther corner of my room or box; but the monkey looking in at every side, put me into such a fright that I wanted presence of mind to conceal myself under the bed, as I might easily have done. After some time spent in peeping, grinning, and chattering, he at last espied me, and reaching one of his paws in at the door, as a cat does when she plays with a mouse, although I often shifted place to avoid him, he at length seized the lappet of my coat (which, being made of that country silk, was very thick and strong), and dragged me out. He took me out in his right fore-foot, and held me as a nurse does a child, just as I have seen the same sort of creature do with a kitten in Europe: and, when I offered to struggle, he squeezed me so hard that I thought it more prudent to submit. I have good reason to believe that he took me for a young one of his own species, by his often stroking my face very gently with his other paw.

In these diversions he was interrupted by a noise at the closet door, as if somebody were opening it; whereupon he suddenly leaped up to the window, at which he had come in, and thence upon the leads and gutters walking upon three legs, and holding me in the fourth, till he clambered up to a roof that was next to ours. I heard Glumdalclitch give a shriek at the moment he was carrying me out. The poor girl was almost distracted. That quarter of the palace was all in an uproar; the servants ran for ladders; the monkey was seen by hundreds in the court, sitting upon the ridge of a building, holding me like a baby in one of his fore-paws: whereat many of the rabble below could not forbear laughing; neither do I think they justly ought to be blamed, for without question, the sight was ridiculous enough to everybody but myself. Some of the people threw up stones, hoping to drive the monkey down; but this was strictly forbidden, or else very probably my brains had been dashed out.

The ladders were now applied, and mounted by several men, which the monkey observing, and finding himself almost encompassed, not being able to make speed enough with his three legs, let me drop on a ridge tile, and made his escape. Here I sat for some time, five hundred yards from the ground, expecting every moment to be blown down by the wind, or to fall by my own giddiness, and come tumbling over and over from the ridge to the eaves; but an honest lad, one of my nurse's footmen, climbed up, and putting me into his breeches-pocket, brought me down safe.

I was so weak and bruised in the sides with the squeezes given me by this odious animal, that I was forced to keep my bed a fortnight. The king, queen, and all the court, sent every day to inquire after my health, and her majesty made me several visits during my sickness. The monkey was killed, and an order made that no such animal should be kept about the palace.

When I attended the king, after my recovery, to return him thanks for his favors, he was pleased to rally me a good deal upon this adventure. He asked me what my thoughts and speculations were while I lay in the monkey's paw. He desired to know what I would have done upon such an occasion in my own country. I told his majesty that in Europe we had no monkeys, except such as were brought for curiosities from other places, and so small, that I could deal with a dozen of them together if they presumed to attack me. And as for that monstrous animal with whom I was so lately engaged (it was, indeed, as large as an elephant) if my fears had suffered me to think so far as to make use of my hanger (looking fiercely, and clapping my hand upon the hilt, as I spoke) when he poked his paw into my chamber, perhaps I should have given him such a wound as would have made him glad to withdraw it with more haste than he put it in. This I delivered in a firm tone, like a person who was jealous lest his courage should be called in question.

However, my speech produced nothing else besides a loud laughter, which all the respect due to his majesty from those about him could not make them contain. This made me reflect how vain an attempt it is for a man to endeavor to do himself honor among those who are out of all degree of equality or comparison with him. And yet I have seen the moral of my own behavior very frequent in England since my return, where a little contemptible varlet,[12] without the least title to birth, person, wit, or common-sense, shall presume to look with importance, and put himself upon a foot with the greatest persons of the kingdom.

I was every day furnishing the court with some ridiculous story; and Glumdalclitch, although she loved me to excess, yet was arch enough to inform the queen whenever I committed any folly that she thought would be diverting to her majesty. The girl, who had been out of order, was carried by her governess to take the air about an hour's distance, or thirty miles from town. They alighted out of the coach near a small footpath in a field, and, Glumdalclitch setting down my travelling-box, I went out of it to walk. There was a pool of mud in the path, and I must needs try my activity by attempting to leap over it. I took a run, but unfortunately jumped short, and found myself just in the middle up to my knees. I waded through with some difficulty, and one of the footmen wiped me as clean as he could with his handkerchief, for I was filthily bemired; and my nurse confined me to my box till we returned home, when the queen was soon informed of what had passed, and the footman spread it about the court; so that all the mirth for some days was at my expense.

---

[67] *Espalier*: a lattice upon which fruit-trees or shrubs are trained.

[68] *Scull*: a short oar.

[69] *Starboard or larboard*: right or left.

[70] *Corking-pin*: a larger-sized pin.

[71] *Stomacher*: a broad belt.

[72] *Varlet*: knave.

CHAPTER VI.

Several Contrivances of the Author to Please the King and Queen. He Shows His Skill in Music. the King Inquires Into the State of England, Which the Author Relates to Him. the King's Observations Thereon.

I used to attend the king's levee[13] once or twice a week, and had often seen him under the barber's hand, which indeed was at first very terrible to behold; for the razor was almost twice as long as an ordinary scythe. His majesty, according to the custom of the country, was only shaved twice a week. I once prevailed on the barber to give me some of the suds or lather, out of which I picked forty or fifty of the strongest stumps of hair, I then took a piece of fine wood and cut it like the back of a comb, making several holes in it at equal distance with as small a needle as I could get from Glumdalclitch. I fixed in the stumps so artificially, scraping and sloping them with my knife towards the points, that I made a very tolerable comb; which was a seasonable supply, my own being so much broken in the teeth that it was almost useless: neither did I know any artist in that country so nice and exact as would undertake to make me another.

And this puts me in mind of an amusement wherein I spent many of my leisure hours. I desired the queen's woman to save for me the combings of her majesty's hair, whereof in time I got a good quantity; and consulting with my friend the cabinet–maker, who had received general orders to do little jobs for me, I directed him to make two chair-frames, no larger than those I had in my box, and then to bore little holes with a fine awl round those parts where I designed the backs and seats; through these holes I wove the strongest hairs I could pick out, just after the manner of cane chairs in England. When they were finished I made a present of them to her majesty, who kept them in her cabinet, and used to shew them for curiosities, as indeed they were the wonder of every one that beheld them. Of these hairs (as I had always a mechanical genius) I likewise made a neat little purse, about five feet long, with her majesty's name deciphered in gold letters, which I gave to Glumdalclitch, by the queen's consent. To say the truth, it was more for show than use, being not of strength to bear the weight of the larger coins, and therefore she kept nothing in it, but some little coins that girls are fond of.

The king, who delighted in music, had frequent concerts at court, to which I was sometimes carried, and set in my box on a table to hear them; but the noise was so great that I could hardly distinguish the tunes. I am confident that all the drums and trumpets of a royal army beating and sounding together just at your ears, could not equal it. My practice was to have my box removed from the place where the performers sat, as far as I could, then to shut the doors and windows of it, and draw

the window–curtains, after which I found their music not disagreeable.

I had learnt in my youth to play a little upon the spinet.[74] Glumdalclitch kept one in her chamber, and a master attended twice a week to teach her. I called it a spinet, because it somewhat resembled that instrument, and was played upon in the same manner.

A fancy came into my head that I would entertain the king and queen with an English tune upon this instrument. But this appeared extremely difficult; for the spinet was nearly sixty feet long, each key being almost a foot wide, so that with my arms extended I could not reach to above five keys, and to press them down required a good smart stroke with my fist, which would be too great a labor, and to no purpose. The method I contrived was this: I prepared two round sticks, about the bigness of common cudgels; they were thicker at one end than the other, and I covered the thicker ends with a piece of mouse's skin, that by rapping on them I might neither damage the tops of the keys nor interrupt the sound. Before the spinet a bench was placed about four feet below the keys, and I was put upon the bench. I ran sideling upon it that way and this as fast as I could, banging the proper keys with my two sticks, and made a shift to play a jig to the great satisfaction of both their majesties; but it was the most violent exercise I ever underwent, and yet I could not strike above sixteen keys, nor consequently play the bass and treble together as other artists do, which was a great disadvantage to my performance.

The king, who, as I before observed, was a prince of excellent understanding, would frequently order that I should be brought in my box, and set upon the table in his closet.[75] He would then command me to bring one of my chairs out of the box, and sit down within three yards distance upon the top of the cabinet, which brought me almost to a level with his face. In this manner I had several conversations with him. I one day took the freedom to tell his majesty that the contempt he discovered towards Europe and the rest of the world did not seem answerable to those excellent qualities of mind that he was master of; that reason did not extend itself with the bulk of the body; on the contrary, we observed in our country that the tallest persons were usually least provided with it. That, among other animals, bees and ants had the reputation of more industry, art, and sagacity than many of the larger kinds; and that, as inconsiderable as he took me to be, I hoped I might live to do his majesty some signal[76] service. The king heard me with attention, and began to conceive a much better opinion of me than he had ever before. He desired I would give him as exact an account of the government of England as I possibly could because, as fond as princes commonly are of their own customs (for he conjectured of other monarchs by my former discourses), he should be glad to hear of anything that might deserve imitation.

Imagine with thyself, courteous reader, how often I then wished for the tongue of Demosthenes or Cicero, that might have enabled me to celebrate the praise of my own dear native country, in a style equal to its merits and felicity.

"THE MOST VIOLENT EXERCISE I EVER UNDERWENT."

I began my discourse by informing his majesty that our dominions consisted of two islands, which composed three mighty kingdoms, under one sovereign, besides our plantations in America. I dwelt long upon the fertility of our soil and the temperature of our climate. I then spoke at large upon the constitution of an English parliament, partly made up of an illustrious body, called the House of Peers, persons of the noblest blood and of the most ancient and ample patrimonies. I described that extraordinary care always taken of their education in arts and arms, to qualify them for being counsellors both to the king and kingdom; to have a share in the legislature; to be members of the highest court of judicature, from whence there could be no appeal; and to be champions always ready for the defence of their prince and country, by their valor, conduct, and fidelity. That these were the ornament and bulwark of the kingdom, worthy followers of their most renowned ancestors, whose honor had been the reward of their virtue, from which their posterity were never once known to degenerate. To these were joined several holy persons, as part of that assembly, under the title of bishops, whose peculiar business it is to take care of religion, and those who instruct the people therein. These were searched and sought out through the whole nation, by the prince and his wisest counsellors, among such of the priesthood as were most deservedly distinguished by the sanctity of their lives and the depth of their erudition, who were indeed the spiritual fathers of the clergy and the people.

That the other part of the parliament consisted of an assembly, called the House of Commons, who were all principal gentlemen, *freely* picked and culled out by the people themselves, for their great abilities and love of their country, to represent the wisdom of the whole nation. And that these two bodies made up the most august assembly in Europe, to whom, in conjunction with the prince, the whole legislature is committed.

I then descended to the courts of justice, over which the judges, those venerable sages and interpreters of the law, presided, for determining the disputed rights and properties of men, as well as for the punishment of vice and protection of innocence. I mentioned the prudent management of our treasury, the valor and achievements of our forces by sea and land. I computed the number of our people, by reckoning how many millions there might be of each religious sect or political party among us. I did not omit even our sports and pastimes, or any other particular, which I thought might redound to the honor of my country. And I finished all with a brief historical account of affairs and events in England for about a hundred years past.

This conversation was not ended under five audiences, each of several hours; and the king heard the whole with great attention, frequently taking notes of what I spoke, as well as memorandums of what questions he intended to ask me.

When I had put an end to these long discourses, his majesty, in a sixth audience, consulting his notes, proposed many doubts, queries, and objections, upon every article. He asked what methods were used to cultivate the minds and bodies of our young nobility, and in what kind of business they commonly spent the first and teachable part of their lives? What course was taken to supply that assembly when any noble family became extinct? What qualifications were necessary in those who are to be created new lords; whether the humor of the prince, a sum of money to a court lady as a prime minister, or a design of strengthening a party opposite to the public interest, ever happened to be motives in those advancements? What share of knowledge these lords had in the laws of their country, and how they came by it, so as to enable them to decide the properties of their fellow-subjects in the last resort? Whether they were always so free from avarice, partialities, or want, that a bribe or some other sinister view could have no place among them? Whether those holy lords I spoke of were always promoted to that rank upon account of their knowledge in religious matters and the sanctity of their lives; had never been compilers with the times while they were common priests, or slavish prostitute chaplains to some noblemen, whose opinions they continued servilely to follow, after they were admitted into that assembly?

He then desired to know what arts were practised in electing those whom I called commoners; whether a stranger, with a strong purse, might not influence the vulgar voters to choose him before their own landlord, or the most considerable gentleman in the neighborhood? How it came to pass that people were so violently bent upon getting into this assembly, which I allowed to be a great trouble and expense, often to the ruin of their families, without any salary or pension: because this appeared such an exalted strain of virtue and public spirit, that his majesty seemed to doubt it might possibly not be always sincere; and he desired to know whether such zealous gentlemen could have any views of refunding themselves for the charges and trouble they were at, by sacrificing the public good to the designs of a weak and vicious prince, in conjunction with a corrupted ministry? He multiplied his questions, and sifted me thoroughly upon every part of this head, proposing numberless inquiries and objections, which I think it not prudent or convenient to repeat.

Upon what I said in relation to our courts of justice, his majesty desired to be satisfied in several points; and this I was the better able to do, having been formerly almost ruined by a long suit in chancery,[77] which was decreed for me with costs. He asked what time was usually spent in determining between right and wrong, and what degree of expense? Whether advocates and orators had liberty to plead in causes, manifestly known to be unjust, vexatious, or oppressive? Whether party in religion or politics was observed to be of any weight in the scale of justice? Whether those pleading orators were persons educated in the general knowledge of equity, or only in provincial, national, and other local customs? Whether they, or their judges, had any part in penning those laws which they assumed the liberty of interpreting and glossing[78] upon at their pleasure? Whether they had ever, at different times, pleaded for or against the same cause, and cited precedents to prove contrary opinions? Whether they were a rich or a poor corporation? Whether they received any pecuniary reward for pleading or delivering their opinions? And, particularly, whether they were admitted as members in the lower senate?

He fell next upon the management of our treasury, and said he thought my memory had failed me, because I computed our taxes at about five or six millions a year, and, when I came to mention the issues, he found they sometimes amounted to more than double; for the notes he had taken were very particular in this point, because he hoped, as he told me, that the knowledge of our conduct might be useful to him, and he could not be deceived in his calculations. But if what I told him were true, he was still at a loss how a kingdom could run out of its estate like a private person. He asked me who were our creditors, and where we found to pay them. He wondered to hear me talk of such chargeable and expensive wars; that certainly we must be a quarrelsome people, or live among very bad neighbors and that our generals must needs be richer than our kings. He asked what business we had out of our own islands, unless upon the score of trade or treaty, or to defend the coasts with our fleet. Above all, he was amazed to hear me talk of a mercenary standing army in the midst of peace and among a free people. He said if we were governed by our own consent, in the persons of our representatives, he could not imagine of whom we were afraid, or against whom we were to fight; and would hear my opinion, whether a private man's house might not better be defended by himself, his children, and family, than by half-a-dozen rascals, picked up at a venture in the streets for small wages, who might get a hundred times more by cutting their throats?

He laughed at my odd kind of arithmetic (as he was pleased to call it), in reckoning the numbers of our people by a computation drawn from the several sects among us, in religion and politics. He said, he knew no reason why those who entertain opinions prejudicial to the public should be obliged to change, or should not be obliged to conceal them. And as it was tyranny in any government to require the first, so it was weakness not to enforce the second: for a man may be allowed to keep poisons in his closet, but not to vend them about for cordials.

He observed, that among the diversions of our nobility and gentry, I had mentioned gaming: he desired to know at what age this entertainment was usually taken up, and when it was laid down; how much of their time it employed: whether it ever went so high as to affect their fortunes: whether mean, vicious people, by their dexterity in that art, might not arrive at great riches, and sometimes keep our very nobles in dependence, as well as habituate them to vile companions, wholly take them from the improvement of their minds, and force them, by the losses they received, to learn and practise that infamous dexterity upon others?

He was perfectly astonished with the historical account I gave him of our affairs during the last century, protesting it was only a heap of conspiracies, rebellions, murders, massacres, revolutions, banishments, the very worst effects that avarice, faction, hypocrisy, perfidiousness, cruelty, rage, madness, hatred, envy, lust, malice, and ambition, could produce.

His majesty, in another audience, was at the pains to recapitulate the sum of all I had spoken; compared the questions he made with the answers I had given; then taking me into his hands, and stroking me gently, delivered himself in these words which I shall never forget, nor the manner he spoke them in: "My little friend Grildrig, you have made a most admirable panegyric upon your country; you have clearly proved that ignorance, idleness, and vice are the proper ingredients for qualifying a legislator; that laws are best explained, interpreted, and applied by those whose interest and abilities lie in perverting, confounding, and eluding them. I observe among you some lines of an institution, which in its original might have been tolerable, but these half erased, and the rest wholly blurred and blotted by corruptions. It doth not appear, from all you have said, how any one perfection is required towards the procurement of any one station among you; much less that men are ennobled on account of their virtue, that priests are advanced for their piety or learning, soldiers for their conduct or valor, judges for their integrity, senators for the love of their country, or counsellors for their wisdom. As for yourself, continued the king, who have spent the greatest part of your life in travelling, I am well disposed to hope you may hitherto have escaped many vices of your country. But by what I have gathered from your own relation, and the answers I have with much pains wrung and extorted from you, I cannot but conclude the bulk of your natives to be the most pernicious race of little odious vermin that nature ever suffered to crawl upon the surface of the earth."

"YOU HAVE MADE A MOST ADMIRABLE PANEGYRIC."

---

[73] *Levee*: a ceremonious visit received by a distinguished person in the morning.

[74] *Spinet*: a stringed instrument, a forerunner of out piano.

[75] *Closet*: private room.

[76] *Signal*: memorable.

[77] *Chancery*: a high court of equity.

[78] *Glossing*: commenting.

CHAPTER VII

The Author's Love of His Country. He Makes a Proposal of Much Advantage to the King, Which is Rejected. the King's Great Ignorance in Politics. the Learning of That Country Very Imperfect and Confined. the Laws, and Military Affairs, and Parties in the State.

Nothing but an extreme love of truth could have hindered me from concealing this part of my story. It was in vain to discover my resentments, which were always turned into ridicule; and I was forced to rest with patience, while my noble and beloved country was so injuriously treated. I am as heartily sorry as any of my readers can possibly be, that such an occasion was given: but this prince happened to be so curious and inquisitive upon every particular, that it could not consist either with gratitude or good manners, to refuse giving him what satisfaction I was able. Yet this much I may be allowed to say, in my own vindication, that I artfully eluded many of his questions, and gave to every point a more favorable turn, by many degrees, than the strictness of truth would allow. For I have always borne that laudable partiality to my own country, which Dionysius Halicarnassensis[29] with so much justice, recommends to an historian: I would hide the frailties and deformities of my political mother, and place her virtues and beauties in the most advantageous light. This was my sincere endeavor, in those many discourses I had with that monarch, although it unfortunately failed of success.

But great allowances should be given to a king who lives wholly secluded from the rest of the world, and must therefore be altogether unacquainted with the manners and customs that most prevail in other nations: the want of which knowledge will ever produce many prejudices, and a certain narrowness of thinking, from which we and the politer countries of Europe are wholly exempted. And it would be hard indeed, if so remote a prince's notions of virtue and vice were to be offered as a standard for all mankind.

To confirm what I have now said, and farther to show the miserable effects of a confined education, I shall here insert a passage which will hardly obtain belief. In hopes to ingratiate myself farther into his majesty's favor, I told him of an invention discovered between three and four hundred years ago, to make a certain powder into a heap, on which the smallest spark of fire falling would kindle the whole in a moment, although it were as big as a mountain, and make it all fly up in the air together with a noise and agitation greater than thunder. That a proper quantity of this powder rammed into a hollow tube of brass or iron, according to its bigness, would drive a ball of iron or lead with such violence and speed as nothing was able to sustain its force. That the largest balls thus discharged would not only destroy whole ranks of an army at once, but batter the strongest walls to the ground, sink down ships with a thousand men in each to the bottom of the sea; and, when linked together by a chain, would cut through masts and rigging, divide hundreds of bodies in the middle, and lay all waste before them. That we often put this powder into large hollow balls of iron, and discharged them by an engine into some city we were besieging, which would rip up the pavements, tear the houses to pieces, burst and throw splinters on every side, dashing out the brains of all who came near. That I knew the ingredients very well, which were cheap and common; I understood the manner of compounding them, and could direct his workman how to make those tubes of a size proportionable to all other things in his majesty's kingdom, and the largest need not to be above a hundred feet long; twenty or thirty of which tubes, charged with the proper quantity of powder and balls, would batter down the walls of the strongest town in his dominions in a few hours, or destroy the whole metropolis if ever it should pretend to dispute his absolute commands. This I humbly offered to his majesty as a small tribute of acknowledgment, in return for so many marks that I had received of his royal favor and protection.

The king was struck with horror at the description I had given him of those terrible engines, and the proposal I had made. He was amazed, how so impotent and grovelling an insect as I (these were his expressions), could entertain such inhuman ideas, and in so familiar a manner, as to appear wholly unmoved at all the scenes of blood and desolation, which I had painted, as the common effects of those destructive machines, whereof, he said, some evil genius, enemy to mankind, must have been the first contriver. As for himself, he protested, that although few things delighted him so much as new discoveries in art or in nature, yet he would rather lose half his kingdom than be privy to such a secret, which he commanded me, as I valued my life, never to mention any more.

A strange effect of narrow principles and short views! that a prince possessed of every quality which procures veneration, love, and esteem; of strong parts, great wisdom, and profound learning, endowed with admirable talents for government, and almost adored by his subjects, should, from a nice unnecessary scruple, whereof in Europe we can have no conception, let slip an opportunity put into his hands, that would have made him absolute master of the lives, the liberties, and the fortunes of his people. Neither do I say this with the least intention to detract from the many virtues of that excellent king, whose character I am sensible will on this account be very much lessened in the opinion of an English reader; but I take this defect among them to have arisen from their ignorance, by not having hitherto reduced politics into a science, as the more acute wits of Europe have done. For I remember very well, in a discourse one day with the king, when I happened to say there were several thousand books among us, written upon the art of government, it gave him (directly contrary to my intention) a very mean opinion of our understandings. He professed both to abominate and despise all mystery, refinement, and intrigue, either in a prince or a minister. He could not tell what I meant by secrets of state, where an enemy or some rival nation were not in the case. He confined the knowledge of governing within very narrow bounds, to common sense and reason, to justice and lenity, to the speedy determination of civil and criminal causes, with some other obvious topics, which are not worth considering. And he gave it for his opinion, that whoever could make two ears of corn, or two blades of grass to grow upon a spot of ground, where only one grew before, would deserve better of mankind, and do more essential service to his country, than the whole race of politicians put together.

The learning of this people is very defective, consisting only in morality, history, poetry, and mathematics, wherein they must be allowed to excel. But the last of these is wholly applied to what may be useful in life, to the improvement of agriculture, and all mechanical arts; so that among us it would be little esteemed. And as to ideas, entities, abstractions, and transcendentals,[80] I could never drive the least conception into their heads.

No law of that country must exceed in words the number of letters in their alphabet, which consists only in two-and-twenty. But indeed few of them extend even to that length. They are expressed in the most plain and simple terms, wherein those people are not mercurial[81] enough to discover above one interpretation; and to write a comment upon any law is a capital crime. As to the decision of civil causes, or proceedings against criminals, their precedents are so few, that they have little reason to boast of any extraordinary skill in either.

They have had the art of printing, as well as the Chinese, time out of mind: but their libraries are not very large; for that of the king, which is reckoned the largest, doth not amount to above a thousand volumes, placed in a gallery of twelve hundred feet long, from whence I had liberty to borrow what books I pleased. The queen's joiner had contrived in one of Glumdalclitch's rooms, a kind of wooden machine, five-and-twenty feet high, formed like a standing ladder; the steps were each fifty feet long: it was indeed a movable pair of stairs, the lowest end placed at ten feet distance from the wall of the chamber. The book I had a mind to read was put up leaning against the wall: I first mounted to the upper step of the ladder, and turning my face towards the book began at the top of the page, and so walking to the right and left about eight or ten paces, according to the length of the lines, till I had gotten a little below the level of mine eyes, and then descending gradually, till I came to the bottom: after which I mounted again, and began the other page in the same manner, and so turned over the leaf, which I could easily do with both my hands, for it was as thick and stiff as a paste-board, and in the largest folios not above eighteen or twenty feet long.

Their style is clear, masculine, and smooth, but not florid; for they avoid nothing more than multiplying unnecessary words, or using various expressions. I have perused many of their books, especially those in history and morality. Among the rest, I was much diverted with a little old treatise, which always lay in Glumdalclitch's bed-chamber, and belonged to her governess, a grave elderly gentlewoman, who dealt in writings of morality and devotion. The book treats of the weakness of human kind, and is in little esteem, except among the women and the vulgar. However, I was curious to

see what an author of that country could say upon such a subject.

This writer went through all the usual topics of European moralists, showing how diminutive, contemptible, and helpless an animal was man in his own nature; how unable to defend himself from inclemencies of the air, or the fury of wild beasts; how much he was excelled by one creature in strength, by another in speed, by a third in foresight, by a fourth in industry. He added, that nature was degenerated in these latter declining ages of the world, and could now produce only small births, in comparison to those in ancient times. He said, it was very reasonable to think, not only that the species of men were originally much larger, but also, that there must have been giants in former ages; which as it is asserted by history and tradition, so it hath been confirmed by huge bones and skulls, casually dug up in several parts of the kingdom, far exceeding the common dwindled race of man in our days. He argued, that the very laws of nature absolutely required we should have been made in the beginning of a size more large and robust, not so liable to destruction, from every little accident, of a tile falling from a house, or a stone cast from the hand of a boy, or being drowned in a little brook. From this way of reasoning the author drew several moral applications, useful in the conduct of life, but needless here to repeat. For my own part, I could not avoid reflecting, how universally this talent was spread, of drawing lectures in morality, or, indeed, rather matter of discontent and repining, from the quarrels we raise with nature. And I believe, upon a strict inquiry, those quarrels might be shown as ill-grounded among us as they are among that people.

As to their military affairs, they boast that the king's army consists of a hundred and seventy-six thousand foot, and thirty-two thousand horse: if that may be called an army which is made up of tradesmen in the several cities, and farmers in the country, whose commanders are only the nobility and gentry, without pay or reward. They are indeed perfect enough in their exercises, and under very good discipline, wherein I saw no great merit; for how should it be otherwise, where every farmer is under the command of his own landlord, and every citizen under that of the principal men in his own city, chosen after the manner of Venice, by ballot?

I have often seen the militia of Lorbrulgrud drawn out to exercise in a great field, near the city, of twenty miles square. They were in all not above twenty-five thousand foot, and six thousand horse: but it was impossible for me to compute their number, considering the space of ground they took up. A cavalier, mounted on a large steed, might be about ninety feet high. I have seen this whole body of horse, upon a word of command, draw their swords at once, and brandish them in the air. Imagination can figure nothing so grand, so surprising, and so astonishing! it looked as if ten thousand flashes of lightning were darting at the same time from every quarter of the sky.

I was curious to know how this prince, to whose dominions there is no access from any other country, came to think of armies, or to teach his people the practice of military discipline. But I was soon informed, both by conversation and reading their histories: for in the course of many ages, they have been troubled with the same disease to which the whole race of mankind is subject; the nobility often contending for power, the people for liberty, and the king for absolute dominion. All which, however, happily tempered by the laws of that kingdom, have been sometimes violated by each of the three parties, and have more than once occasioned civil wars, the last whereof was happily put an end to by this prince's grandfather, in a general composition;[82] and the militia, then settled with common consent, hath been ever since kept in the strictest duty.

[79] *Dionysius of Halicarnassus* was born about the middle of the first century, B.C.; he endeavored in his history to relieve his Greek countrymen from the mortification they had felt in their subjection to the Romans, and patched up an old legend about Rome being of Greek origin and therefore their "political mother."

[80] *Ideas, entities, abstractions, transcendentals*, words used in that philosophy which deals with thinking, existence, and things beyond the senses.

[81] *Mercurial*: active, spirited.

[82] *Composition*: compact, agreement.

CHAPTER VIII

The King and Queen Make a Progress[83] to the Frontiers. the Author Attends Them. the Manner in Which He Leaves the Country Very Particularly Related. He Returns to England.

I had always a strong impulse that I should sometime recover my liberty, though it was impossible to conjecture by what means, or to form any project with the least hope of succeeding. The ship in which I sailed was the first ever known to be driven within sight of the coast; and the king had given strict orders, that if at any time another appeared, it should be taken ashore, and with all its crew and passengers brought in a tumbrel[84] to Lorbrulgrud. I was treated with much kindness: I was the favorite of a great king and queen, and the delight of the whole court; but it was upon such a footing as ill became the dignity of human kind. I could never forget those domestic pledges I had left behind me. I wanted to be among people with whom I could converse upon even terms, and walk about the streets and fields, without being afraid of being trod to death like a frog or a young puppy. But my deliverance came sooner than I expected, and in a manner not very common: the whole story and circumstances of which I shall faithfully relate.

"SHE HAD SOME FOREBODING."

117

I had now been two years in this country; and about the beginning of the third, Glumdalclitch and I attended the king and queen in a progress to the south coast of the kingdom. I was carried, as usual, in my travelling-box, which, as I have already described, was a very convenient closet of twelve feet wide. And I had ordered a hammock to be fixed by silken ropes from the four corners at the top, to break the jolts, when a servant carried me before him on horseback, as I sometimes desired, and would often sleep in my hammock while we were upon the road. On the roof of my closet, not directly over the middle of the hammock, I ordered the joiner to cut out a hole of a foot square, to give me air in hot weather as I slept, which hole I shut at pleasure with a board that drew backwards and forwards through a groove.

When we came to our journey's end, the king thought proper to pass a few days at a palace he hath near Flanflasnic, a city within eighteen English of the sea-side Glumdalclitch and I were much fatigued, I had gotten a small cold, but the poor girl was so ill as to be confined to her chamber. I longed to see the ocean, which must be the only scene of my escape, if ever it should happen I pretended to be worse than I really was, and desired leave to take the fresh air of the sea with a page, whom I was very fond of, and who had sometimes been trusted with me. I shall never forget with what unwillingness Glumdalclitch consented, nor the strict charge she gave the page[85] to be careful of me, bursting at the same time into a flood of tears, as if she had some foreboding of what was to happen.

The boy took me out in my box about half-an-hour's walk from the palace towards the rocks on the sea-shore. I ordered him to set me down, and lifting up one of my sashes, cast many a wistful melancholy look towards the sea. I found myself not very well, and told the page that I had a mind to take a nap in my hammock, which I hoped would do me good. I got in, and the boy shut the window close down to keep out the cold. I soon fell asleep, and all I can conjecture is, that while I slept, the page, thinking no danger could happen, went among the rocks to look for birds' eggs, having before observed him from my windows searching about, and picking up one or two in the clefts. Be that as it will, I found myself suddenly awaked with a violent pull upon the ring, which was fastened at the top of my box for the conveniency of carriage. I felt my box raised very high in the air, and then borne forward with prodigious speed. The first jolt had like to have shaken me out of my hammock, but afterwards the motion was easy enough. I called out several times, as loud as I could raise my voice, but all to no purpose. I looked towards my windows, and could see nothing but the clouds and sky. I heard a noise just over my head like the clapping of wings, and then began to perceive the woful condition I was in, that some eagle had got the ring of my box in his beak, with an intent to let it fall on a rock like a tortoise in a shell, and then pick out my body and devour it; for the sagacity and smell of this bird enabled him to discover his quarry[86] at a great distance, though better concealed than I could be within a two-inch board.

In a little time I observed the noise and flutter of wings to increase very fast, and my box was tossed up and down like a sign in a windy day. I heard several bangs or buffets, as I thought, given to the eagle (for such I am certain it must have been, that held the ring of my box in his beak), and then all on a sudden felt myself falling perpendicularly down for above a minute, but with such incredible swiftness, that I almost lost my breath. My fall was stopped by a terrible squash,[87] that sounded louder to my ears than the cataract of Niagara; after which I was quite in the dark for another minute, and then my box began to rise so high that I could see light from the tops of the windows. I now perceived I was fallen into the sea. My box, by the weight of my body, the goods that were in, and the broad plates of iron fixed for strength at the four corners of the top and bottom, floated about five feet deep in the water. I did then, and do now suppose, that the eagle which flew away with my box was pursued by two or three others, and forced to let me drop while he defended himself against the rest, who hoped to share in the prey. The plates of iron fastened at the bottom of the box (for those were the strongest) preserved the balance while it fell, and hindered it from being broken on the surface of the water. Every joint of it was well grooved, and the door did not move on hinges, but up and down like a sash, which kept my closet so tight that very little water came in. I got with much difficulty out of my hammock, having first ventured to draw back my slip-board on the roof already mentioned, contrived on purpose to let in air, for want of which I found myself almost stifled.

How often did I then wish myself with my dear Glumdalclitch, from whom one single hour had so far divided me. And I may say with truth that in the midst of my own misfortunes I could not forbear lamenting my poor nurse, the grief she would suffer for my loss, the displeasure of the queen, and the ruin of her fortune. Perhaps many travellers have not been under greater difficulties and distress than I was at juncture, expecting every moment to see my box dashed to pieces, or at least overset by the first violent blast or rising wave. A breach in one single pane of glass would have been immediate death; nor could anything have preserved the windows but the strong lattice-wires placed on the outside against accidents in travelling. I saw the water ooze in at several crannies, although the leaks were not considerable, and I endeavored to stop them as well as I could, I was not able to lift up the roof of my closet, which otherwise I certainly should have done, and sat on the top of it, where I might at least preserve myself some hours longer, than by being shut up (as I may call it) in the hold. Or, if I escaped these dangers for a day or two, what could I expect but a miserable death of cold and hunger? I was four hours under these circumstances, expecting, and indeed wishing, every moment to be my last.

I have already told the reader that there were two strong staples fixed upon that side of my box which had no window, and into which the servant who used to carry me on horseback would put a leathern belt, and buckle it about his waist. Being in this disconsolate state, I heard, or at least thought I heard, some kind of grating noise on that side of my box where the staples were fixed, and soon after I began to fancy that the box was pulled or towed along in the sea, for I now and then felt a sort of tugging which made the waves rise near the tops of my windows, leaving me almost in the dark. This gave me some faint hopes of relief, although I was not able to imagine how it could be brought about. I ventured to unscrew one of my chairs, which were always fastened to the floor, and having made a hard shift to screw it down again directly under the slipping board that I had lately opened, I mounted on the chair, and putting my mouth as near as I could to the hole, I called for help in a loud voice and in all the languages I understood. I then fastened my handkerchief to a stick I usually carried, and thrusting it up the hole, waved it several times in the air, that if any boat or ship were near, the seamen might conjecture some unhappy mortal to be shut up in the box.

I found no effect from all I could do, but plainly perceived my closet to be moved along; and in the space of an hour or better, that side of the box where the staples were and had no window struck against something that was hard. I apprehended it to be a rock, and found myself tossed more than ever. I plainly heard a noise upon the cover of my closet like that of a cable, and the grating of it as it passed through the ring. I then found myself hoisted up by degrees, at least three feet higher than I was before. Whereupon I again thrust up my stick and handkerchief, calling for help till I was almost hoarse. In return to which I heard a great shout repeated three times, giving me such transports of joy as are not to be conceived but by those who feel them. I now heard a trampling over my head, and somebody calling through the hole with a loud voice in the English tongue. "If there be anybody below, let them speak." I answered I was an Englishman, drawn by ill fortune into the greatest calamity that ever any creature underwent, and begged by all that was moving to be delivered out of the dungeon I was in. The voice replied I was safe, for my box was fastened to their ship; and the carpenter should immediately come and saw a hole in the cover, large enough to pull me out. I answered that was needless, and would take up too much time, for there was no more to be done, but let one of the crew put his finger into the ring, and take the box out of the sea into the ship, and so into the captain's cabin. Some of them upon hearing me talk so wildly thought I was mad; others laughed; for indeed it never came into my head that I was now got among people of my own stature and strength. The carpenter came, and in a few minutes sawed a passage about four feet square, then let down a small ladder upon which I mounted, and from thence was taken into the ship in a very weak condition.

"SOMEBODY CALLING ... IN THE ENGLISH TONGUE."

The sailors were all in amazement, and asked me a thousand questions, which I had no inclination to answer. I was equally confounded at the sight of so many pygmies, for such I took them to be, after having so long accustomed mine eyes to the monstrous objects I had left. But the captain, Mr. Thomas Wilcocks, an honest, worthy Shropshire man, observing I was ready to faint, took me into his cabin, gave me a cordial to comfort me, and made me turn in upon his own bed, advising me to take a little rest, of which I had great need. Before I went to sleep, I gave him to understand that I had some valuable furniture in my box, too good to be lost; a fine hammock, a handsome two chairs, a table, and a cabinet. That my closet was hung on all sides, or rather quilted, with silk and cotton: that if he would let one of the crew bring my closet into

121

his cabin, I would open it there before him, and show him my goods. The captain, hearing me utter these absurdities, concluded I was raving: however (I suppose to pacify me), he promised to give orders as I desired, and going upon deck, sent some of his men down into my closet, from whence (as I afterwards found) they drew up all my goods, and stripped off the quilting; but the chairs, cabinet, and bedstead, being screwed to the floor, were much damaged by the ignorance of the seamen, who tore them up by force. Then they knocked off some of the boards for the use of the ship, and when they had got all they had a mind for, let the hull drop into the sea, which, by reason of so many breaches made in the bottom and sides, sunk to rights.[88] And indeed I was glad not to have been a spectator of the havoc they made; because I am confident it would have sensibly touched me, by bringing former passages into my mind, which I had rather forgotten.

I slept some hours, but was perpetually disturbed with dreams of the place I had left, and the dangers I had escaped. However, upon waking, I found myself much recovered. It was now about eight o'clock at night, and the captain ordered supper immediately, thinking I had already fasted too long. He entertained me with great kindness, observing me not to look wildly, or talk inconsistently; and when we were left alone, desired I would give him a relation of my travels, and by what accident I came to be set adrift in that monstrous wooden chest.

He said that about twelve o'clock at noon, as he was looking through his glass, he spied it at a distance, and thought it was a sail, which he had a mind to make[89], being not much out of his course, in hopes of buying some biscuit, his own beginning to fall short. That upon coming nearer and finding his error, he sent out his long-boat to discover what it was; that his men came back in a fright, swearing they had seen a swimming-house. That he laughed at their folly, and went himself in the boat, ordering his men to take a strong cable along with them. That the weather being calm, he rowed round me several times, observed my windows and wire-lattices that defenced them. That he discovered two staples upon one side, which was all of boards, without any passage for light. He then commanded his men to row up to that side, and fastening a cable to one of the staples, ordered them to tow my chest (as they called it) towards the ship. When it was there, he gave directions to fasten another cable to the ring fixed in the cover, and to raise up my chest with pulleys, which all the sailors were not able to do above two or three feet. He said they saw my stick and handkerchief thrust out of the hole, and concluded that some unhappy man must be shut up in the cavity. I asked whether he or the crew had seen any prodigious birds in the air about the time he first discovered me? to which he answered, that, discoursing this matter with the sailors while I was asleep, one of them said he had observed three eagles flying towards the north, but remarked nothing of their being larger than the usual size, which I suppose must be imputed to the great height they were at; and he could not guess the reason of my question. I then asked the captain how far he reckoned we might be from land?

He said, by the best computation he could make, we were at least a hundred leagues. I assured him that he must be mistaken by almost half, for I had not left the country from whence I came above two hours before I dropt into the sea. Whereupon he began again to think that my brain was disturbed, of which he gave me a hint, and advised me to go to bed in a cabin he had provided. I assured him I was well refreshed with his good entertainment and company, and as much in my senses as ever I was in my life.

He then grew serious, and desired to ask me freely whether I were not troubled in mind by the consciousness of some enormous crime, for which I was punished by the command of some prince, by exposing me in that chest, as great criminals in other countries have been forced to sea in a leaky vessel without provisions; for although he should be sorry to have taken so ill a man into his ship, yet he would engage his word to set me safe ashore in the first port where we arrived. He added that his suspicions were much increased by some very absurd speeches I had delivered, at first to his sailors, and afterwards to himself, in relation to my closet chest, as well as by my odd looks and behavior while I was at supper.

I begged his patience to hear me tell my story, which I faithfully did, from the last time I left England to the moment he first discovered me. And as truth always forceth its way into rational minds, so this honest worthy gentleman, who had some tincture of learning and very good sense, was immediately convinced of my candor and veracity. But, farther to confirm all I had said, I entreated him to give order that my cabinet should be brought, of which I had the key in my pocket (for he had already informed me how seamen disposed of my closet). I opened it in his own presence, and showed him the small collection of rarities I made in the country from whence I had been so strangely delivered. There was the comb I had contrived out of the stumps of the king's beard. There was a collection of needles and pins, from a foot to half a yard long; four wasps' stings, like joiners' tacks; some combings of the queen's hair; a gold ring, which one day she made me a present of in a most obliging manner, taking it from her little finger and throwing it over my head like a collar. I desired the captain would please to accept this ring in return of his civilities, which he absolutely refused. Lastly I desired him to see the breeches I had then on, which were made of a mouse's skin.

I could force nothing upon him but a footman's tooth, which I observed him to examine with great curiosity, and found he had a fancy for it. He received it with abundance of thanks, more than such a trifle could deserve. It was drawn by an unskilful surgeon, in a mistake, from one of Glumdalclitch's men, who was affected with the toothache, but it was as sound as any in his head. I got it cleaned, and put it in my cabinet. It was about a foot long, and four inches in diameter.

The captain was very well satisfied with this plain relation I had given him, and said he hoped when we returned to England I would oblige the world by putting it on paper, and making it public. My answer was, that I thought we were already overstocked with books of travels; that nothing could now pass which was not extraordinary; wherein I doubted some authors less consulted truth than their own vanity, or interest, or the diversion of ignorant readers, that my story could contain little besides common events, without those ornamental descriptions of strange plants, trees, birds, and other animals; or of the barbarous customs and idolatry of savage people, with which most writers abound. However, I thanked him for his good opinion, and promised to take the matter into my thoughts.

He said he wondered at one thing very much, which was, to hear me speak so loud, asking me whether the king or queen of that country were thick of hearing. I told him it was what I had been used to for above two years past, and that I wondered as much at the voices of him and his men, who seemed to me only to whisper, and yet I could hear them well enough. But when I spoke in that country, it was like a man talking in the street to another looking out from the top of a steeple, unless when I was placed on a table, or held in any person's hand. I told him I had likewise observed another thing, that when I first got into the ship, and the sailors stood all about me, I thought they were the most contemptible little creatures I had ever beheld. For indeed, while I was in that prince's country, I could never endure to look in a glass, after my eyes had been accustomed to such prodigious objects, because the comparison gave me so despicable a conceit of myself. The captain said that while we were at supper he observed me to look at everything with a sort of wonder, and that I often seemed hardly able to contain my laughter, which he knew not well how to take, but imputed it to some disorder in my brain. I answered, it was very true, and I wondered how I could forbear, when I saw his dishes of the size of a silver threepence, a leg of pork hardly a mouthful, a cup not so big as a nut-shell, and so I went on, describing the rest of his household stuff and provisions after the same manner. For although the queen had ordered a little equipage of all things necessary for me, while I was in her service, yet my ideas were wholly taken up with what I saw on every side of me, and I winked at my own littleness, as people do at their own faults. The captain understood my raillery very well, and merrily replied that he did not observe my stomach so good, although I had fasted all day; and, continuing in his mirth, protested he would have gladly given a hundred pounds to have seen my closet in the eagle's bill, and afterwards in its fall from so great a height into the sea; which would certainly have been a most astonishing object, worthy to have the description of it transmitted to future ages: and the comparison of Phaeton[30] was so obvious, that he could not forbear applying it, although I did not much admire the conceit.

"MY DAUGHTER KNEELED BUT I COULD NOT SEE HER"

The captain having been at Tonquin, was, in his return to England, driven northeastward, to the latitude of 44 degrees, and of longitude 143. But meeting a trade-wind two days after I came on board him, we sailed southward a long time, and, coasting New Holland, kept our course west-south-west, and then south-south-west, till we doubled the Cape of Good Hope. Our voyage was very prosperous, but I shall not trouble the reader with a journal of it. The captain called in at one or two ports, and sent in his long-boat for provisions and fresh water, but I never went out of the ship till we came into the Downs, which was on the third day of June, 1706, about nine months after my escape. I offered to leave pay goods in security for payment of my freight, but the captain protested he would not receive one farthing. We took a kind leave of each other, and I made him promise he would come to see me at my house in Redriff. I hired a horse and guide for five shillings, which I borrowed of the captain.

As I was on the road, observing the littleness of the houses—the trees, the cattle, and the people, I began to think myself in Lilliput. I was afraid of trampling on every traveller I met, and often called aloud to have them stand out of the way, so that I had like to have gotten one or two broken heads for my impertinence.

When I came to my own house, for which I was forced to inquire, one of the servants opened the door, I bent down to go in (like a goose under a gate), for fear of striking my head. My wife ran out to embrace me, but I stooped lower than her knees, thinking she could otherwise never be able to reach my mouth. My daughter kneeled to ask my blessing, but I could not see her till she arose, having been so long used to stand with my head and eyes erect to above sixty feet; and then I went to take her up with one hand by the waist. I looked down upon the servants, and one or two friends who were in the house, as if they had been pygmies, and I a giant. I told my wife she had been too thrifty, for I found she had starved herself and her daughter to nothing. In short, I behaved myself so unaccountably, that they were all of the captain's opinion when he first saw me, and concluded I had lost my wits. This I mention as an instance of the great power of habit and prejudice.

In a little time, I and my family and friends came to a right understanding: but my wife protested I should never go to sea any more; although my evil destiny so ordered, that she had not power to hinder me, as the reader may know hereafter. In the meantime I here conclude the second part of my unfortunate voyages.

---

[83] *Progress:* an old term for the travelling of the sovereign to different parts of his country.

[84] *Tumbrel:* a rough cart.

[85] *Page:* a serving-boy, and especially one who waits on a person of rank.

[86] *Quarry:* prey.

[87] *Squash:* shock, concussion.

[88] *To rights* speedily.

[89] *To make* To get alongside.

[90] *Phaeton* a son of Apollo who was dashed into the river Endanus for his foolhardiness in attempting to drive the steeds of the sun for one day.

Printed in Great Britain
by Amazon

33224943R00078